LIAM O'FLAHERTY:
the Unromantic Seanchaí

張婉麗
Ann Wan-lih Chang, Ph.D.

封面設計：實踐大學教務處出版組

For my father

出 版 心 語

　　近年來，全球數位出版蓄勢待發，美國從事數位出版的業者超過百家，亞洲數位出版的新勢力也正在起飛，諸如日本、中國大陸都方興未艾，而臺灣卻被視為數位出版的處女地，有極大的開發拓展空間。植基於此，本組自民國 93 年 9 月起，即醞釀規劃以數位出版模式，協助本校專任教師致力於學術出版，以激勵本校研究風氣，提昇教學品質及學術水準。

　　在規劃初期，調查得知秀威資訊科技股份有限公司是採行數位印刷模式並做數位少量隨需出版〔POD＝Print on Demand〕（含編印銷售發行）的科技公司，亦為中華民國政府出版品正式授權的 POD 數位處理中心，尤其該公司可提供「免費學術出版」形式，相當符合本組推展數位出版的立意。隨即與秀威公司密集接洽，雙方就數位出版服務要點、數位出版申請作業流程、出版發行合約書以及出版合作備忘錄等相關事宜逐一審慎研擬，歷時 9 個月，至民國 94 年 6 月始告順利簽核公布。

　　執行迄今逾 2 年，承蒙本校謝董事長孟雄、謝校長宗興、劉教務長麗雲、藍教授秀璋以及秀威公司宋總經理政坤等多位長官給予本組全力的支持與指導，本校諸多教師亦身體力行，主動提供學術專著委由本組協助數位出版，數量達 20 本，在此一併致上最誠摯的謝意。諸般溫馨滿溢，將是挹注本組持續推展數位出版的最大動力。

　　本出版團隊由葉立誠組長、王雯珊老師、賴怡勳老師三人為組合，以極其有限的人力，充分發揮高效能的團隊精神，合作無間，各司統籌策劃、協商研擬、視覺設計等職掌，在精益求精的前提下，至望弘揚本校實踐大學的校譽，具體落實出版機能。

實踐大學教務處出版組　謹識
2009 年 3 月

CONTENTS

Acknowledgments

Firstly the greatest gratitude from my heart must go to my partner Michael for his support and patience, and for his hard work of proofreading numerous pages for me over the years while I was working on my Ph.D. dissertation and this book. I appreciate in particular his understanding and consideration regarding the ongoing difficult circumstances we have experienced since I was appointed the position of the head of Applied English Department by Shih-chien University, Kaohiung Campus in 2007. I also would like to give my words of thanks to my father, who supported me financially against all odds over the years when I pursued my Ph.D. in UK. I also owe much to the librarians in Special Collections at the Queen's Main Library, the Library of the University of Ulster and the Shih-chien University, where I have obtained most of the information valuable and useful to this book.

Abbreviation of Story Collections

The publication date given parenthetically is the edition used in this book.   Please see *Works Cited* for full bibliographical details.

DL: *Dúil* (1962)

MS: *More Short Stories* (1971)

MT: *The Mountain Tavern* (1929)

PR: *The Pedlar's Revenge and Other Stories* (1996)

SL: *The Stories of Liam O'Flaherty* (1956)

SP: *Spring Sowing* (1927)

SS: *Selected Short Stories* (1970)

TL: *Two Lovely Beasts* (1948)

TT: *The Tent* (1926)

WS: *The Wild Swan and Other Stories* (1932)

Prologue:
The Artist and His Art

A Man with a Divided Self

Liam O'Flaherty (1896-1984) was a man who belonged to two periods. He was born in the pre-modern age and died in the post-modern period. Though he lived to be 88, his literary life was a short one for a writer. Liam O'Flaherty did not produce anything new and had not attracted much notice in his last thirty years. His life was, as an old man, silent and lonely, in sharp contrast with his active and prolific life in his 20s and 30s, when he published most of his novels, wrote over a hundred well-received short stories, and made contributions continuously to newspapers, magazines and journals. Interestingly his primary ambition to be a novelist turned out to be disappointing while, to his surprise, his reputation has been built largely on his short stories instead. As a writer he did not take that genre seriously and nor invest as much as in it as in his novels. In fact, his short stories render a kaleidoscopic and profound literary vision of a world greatly praised by his contemporaries, such as Seán Ó Faoláin (1900-1991) and Frank O'Connor (1903-1966). Indeed O'Connor argues that Liam O'Flaherty is "most masterful as a writer of short stories." [1] His stories representing life and reality on the primitive, barren and lonely Aran Islands on the edge of the civilized world are thought to embody universal feelings, the beauty and magic of the Creator, nature.   Nature, like the sea, is so vast, profound and unpredictable; it can be both benevolent and malevolent.

Liam O'Flaherty was indeed a man with a divided and contradictory self.   He was never confined to any form of ideology or authority.   He tried to avoid any conformity in the style of his writings as he declared that he had no style and did not want any style, and thus he refused to have a style because "style is artificial and vulgar" (O'Flaherty, <u>Letters</u> 81).   Yet his works were sometimes considered to be carefully refined pieces of craftsmanship; he apparently refined them just because they might be more fit for publication.   He is consistent in one attitude only, his rejection of the conformity of the Roman Catholic Church.   He was not an atheist after all, though he claimed to be, but he hated established denominational institutions and dogmatism on the grounds that the Church represses and hinders the active flows of life force and passions, both of which are the essence of life, and without which life is dull and dying.   Mankind is but a species of animal, who must keep in harmony with nature and other creatures, unlike the Nietzchean superman.   In this respect O'Flaherty is also to be viewed as one of the pioneers among his contemporaries to be concerned about the importance of ecology in the modern world (O'Connor 1972, 47).

His art of creation came from the conflicting forces in his mind. As Angeline Kelly says in her introduction to O'Flaherty's collection of short stories <u>The Pedlar's Revenge</u> (14-5):

All art must come from the inner contradiction from the artists which continue to present themselves in endless succession like humpbacked waves drawn up by the moon of his perpetual quest. This true artist is incapable of revealing himself fully because the deep philosophic analysis necessary for this would impoverish the seedbed of intuitive impulse upon which his creative hunger feeds.

Liam O'Flaherty has the quality of an artist in that recurring energies drive him to work.   To fully understand Liam O'Flaherty and his work, it is best to start from the place where he was born and reared: Inishmore, the biggest of the Aran Islands, for the environment played a large part in moulding the artist as well as his art.

Born into a large poor peasant family in 1896 at Gort na gCapall on Inishmore, off the coast of County Galway, Liam O'Flaherty inherited the ferocious and primitive half of his personality from his father's people the O'Flahertys, said to be a powerful clan on the Aran Islands in the 15th century, and his soft, tender and emotional half from his mother's side, Ganlys, whose family originally came from Ulster to build a lighthouse on Aran.   The marriage of his parents was a romantic elopement, and a scenario reenacted a generation later by Liam O'Flaherty himself when he ran away with a historian's wife, who later became his own wife and bore him the daughter Pegeen. His father was a man with a rebellious spirit, a Fenian and active in the mass movements such as on the issue of land struggle on Aran.   In contrast, his tender mother opened the magic world of the wilderness to his eyes and showed him the ancient power of storytelling in the open space of the mountains, valleys and trees.   Though Gaelic was the common language of his neighbours, Liam O'Flaherty was

expected to speak English at home, by his father's wish.   His
relationship with Gaelic and the Aran Islands remained significant and
paradoxical (Costello 13).[2]

Liam O'Flaherty embodies the recurring ambivalence still
existing in the nature of the native Aran islanders: Gaelic and English,
Pagan coexisting with Christian, sexism versus matriarchy, politics and
anti-politics, tragedy and comedy, the struggle of life and death
(Cahalan 1988, 11).   An episode in his childhood marked his talented
imagination and premature sensitivity in his personality.   He started
at the Oatquarter School when he was six.   One day in class he made
up a story with a vivid description of his neighbour murdering his wife
and managing to bury her.   The plot horrified his teacher and his
mother and he was punished for his temerity.   Liam O'Flaherty later
claimed that this early experience in childhood taught him to hide his
private world, the dark half, and left him with a divided self in his
personality:

> The one wept with my mother and felt ashamed of his secret
> mind ... and began to dream of greatness.   And as my mind
> grew strong and defiant, I became timid and sensitive in my
> relationship with the people about me.   I became prone to
> dreaming quick at my schooling, ashamed of vulgar profanity
> and rowdy conduct.[3]

The occurrence of the boycott initiated by the parish priest in
Inishmore in his childhood led to Liam O'Flaherty's anti-clerical
attitude for much of his life.   Even so, his mother still hoped her

bright younger son might become a priest, and he was sent to Rockwell College in Tipperary to receive the necessary formal education. It seemed to be customary, in Catholic rural Ireland at this time, for the intelligent boy of a poor family to enter the priesthood (Jefferson 8).

Instead, O'Flaherty became a *spoiled priest*, and then he transferred to Blackrock College in Co. Dublin where he won a scholarship to University College Dublin (Cahalan 1988, 186). He did not complete his degree at University College Dublin but left to join the Irish Guards of the British Army in 1915 under the alias William Ganly, the name of his uncle and godfather (Costello 27). The horrific experience of war was important to Liam O'Flaherty, for he witnessed the killing and bloodshed of the war at first hand, and he himself was seriously wounded and shell-shocked in 1917. After a year's medical treatment he was discharged from hospital, and was invalided out of the army with a severe case of *melancholia acuta* (Sheeran 67).

Following his release from the army, he wandered aimlessly through a variety of countries without a profitable occupation after the traumatic experience, however O'Flaherty embarked upon a writing career, with the encouragement of his brother Tom who lived in Boston. He went to London, full of fury and hatred of the English, and wanted to write some sensational stories in the city. He was advised by one of his readers at Jonathan Cape, Edward Garnett (1869-1937), who was a father figure to him, to write about something that he had already been familiar with rather than something he knew nothing about. Liam O'Flaherty took the advice, and became well-known for his short stories (Cahalan 1988, 186).

H. E. Bates describes what had happened between them in his book on Edward Garnett (47):

> O'Flaherty had arrived in London with a firebrand swagger, a fine talent and a headful of rebellious fury about the English and had sat down to write pieces of episodic violence about London, which he hardly knew at all.   Garnett promptly and rightly sent him back to Ireland to write about seagulls and congers, a peasant's cow and the flight of a blackbird, and he at once produced sketches of the most delicate feeling and visual brilliance that few, even among the Irish have equalled.

O'Flaherty's first novel, Thy Neighbour's Wife, was published by Jonathan Cape in 1923 on the recommendation of Garnett.   The 1920s to 1930s were an intensely productive but also turbulent period.   Liam O'Flaherty got involved in social movements, finally left Ireland, travelled and moved from one country to another, going to London, France, South America and Russia, where he eventually became disillusioned with Communism, an experience recounted in his autobiography I Went to Russia (1931).   In the meantime he broke off with his fiancée Miss Casey and began an affair with a married woman, Margaret Barrington (d. 1982), who eventually became his wife and mother to his daughter, Pegeen.   At this time he suffered financial difficulties and other stresses which precipitated nervous breakdowns.   After he separated from his wife and daughter in 1932, he moved to stay in California for a year, where he met Kitty Harding Tailer (d. 1990) the woman who became his companion for the remainder of his life.

1937 saw the famous film version of his novel The Informer (1925) directed by Liam O'Flaherty's cousin John Ford. This became his best known work to the popular masses. After the publication of his collection of short stories in Irish, Dúil in 1953, he published no more. As the conflicting forces which had dogged his mind diminished and his creative power for art seemed to peter out to a certain degree, Liam O'Flaherty lived a more peaceful and tranquil later life (Sheeran 67). He died at the age of 88 in Dublin in 1984, and the once anti-clerical rebel was said to have become reconciled with the Catholic Church by Fr Dermod McCarthy of the Pro-Cathedral (Costello 113-4).

Spontaneous Overflow of Powerful Feelings from Aran

As a natural rebel, Liam O'Flaherty actually made a distinctive contribution to the reversal of Celtic Twilight literary fashion in his own time. Leading literary figures in the latter group, such as the poet W. B. Yeats (1865-1939) and the novelist George Moore (1852-1933), had visited Inishmore before Liam O'Flaherty was born in 1896, and afterwards they started a romantic movement in Irish literature, involving the idealization of the past, and seeking fresh inspiration from the ancient tradition. The movement came to be commonly known as the Irish Literary Revival or the Irish Renaissance, and gave birth to a flowering epoch of modern Irish literature at the end of the last and beginning of the current century. O'Flaherty, on the contrary, wrote about his birthplace, the Aran Islands, in a different manner from that of

Yeats or John Millington Synge (1871-1909) who visited the Aran Islands in 1897 before he wrote his famous controversial works <u>The Aran Islands</u> (1907) and plays like "Riders to the Sea" (1904) and "The Playboy of the Western World" (1907) etc.[4]   To Liam O'Flaherty none of the above-mentioned *outsiders* knew more about the peasant's life on the Aran Islands than he owing to the fact that he came from a peasant background, with which he still identified himself in his later life, and he thus presented his own deeper insight into the reality of the life in the west of Ireland (Costello 14).

He always maintained his empathy with the poor people, and his belief in Communism may have been due to his own previous experience having witnessed and been through the hardship and poverty of life in his childhood.   Unlike one of his contemporaries, the Irish poet Máirtín Ó Direáin (1910-1988), who came from the same hometown as O'Flaherty, Inishmore of the Aran Islands, O'Flaherty did not involve their Gaelic enthusiasm and romanticism in the Gaelic revival movement emerging in the late 19th century.[5]

O'Flaherty's works are sometimes described as being melodramatic and inconsistent in character and styles.   His attempt to probe into the intellectual and psychological complexity of human beings is generally thought to be rather feeble, but he is superb when he depicts the elemental reactions and instincts of living creatures including mankind (O'Brien 1973, 95-7).

Frank O'Connor once quoted George Russell as saying: "When O'Flaherty thinks, he's a goose, when he feels, he's a genius" (O'Connor 1962, 38).   His short stories are less criticized in this respect because of his spontaneous overflow of the powerful feelings that came from his own experience and his observation of the order of nature that surrounded him.   The fury and discontent of the characters with a *blackened soul* in most of his novels gave way to a state of calm surface of mind, which Zneimer described as light whose surface is cold and shimmering but with profundity (Zneimer 146).   In his animal world he seems to find something that resembles his ideal beauty (O'Brien 1973, 95).

Simplicity is the hallmark of O'Flaherty's stories.   They seem to bear no complex symbols, characterization, narration and philosophy, and even the plot of the stories is short and easily readable.   They are quite direct descriptive narratives.   Some modern new critics tend to analyse literary texts on their own terms but in the light of a writer's experience.   This may risk misreading and misleading to a confusion because Liam O'Flaherty's works are sometimes autobiographical and very personal and may therefore not have been given much attention and evaluation from critics.

O'Flaherty's achievement as a short story writer is, however, highly acclaimed.   He is considered one of the greatest in this genre of his time, and he is also a pioneer in writing dealing with ecological issues that echoes the current waves of global movements, the care of animals and environment and a return to a simple way of life and nature.   With a kind of Rousseauean romanticism Liam O'Flaherty admires the simplicity and nobility found in wildlife and in a peasant's life, hard but energetic because the energy is an intensity of life, the opposite of death.[6]   He is often associated with ancient Gaelic literary tradition in manipulating the storyteller's narration in his stories.   William Troy viewed the qualities in his work as saying:

> He (Liam O'Flaherty) is closer to the unknown writers of the early Gaelic folk literature than to any of his contemporaries. He is less the product of any modern school than of that period when European culture had not yet entirely lost its innocence.[7]

Some of his stories are meant to be read and to be told like bedtime stories.   Liam O'Flaherty inherited and displayed the influence of the oral tradition of the ancient Gaelic literary heritage in the development of his literary career, but some critics such as Vivian Mercier argues that his stories are better for the eyes than for the ears (Mercier 1964, 98-116).

Even so, there is no doubt of the impact made upon him by the vivid story-telling tradition by his mother and folks in the village, where the oral tradition still prevails.   His stories are also rich in images, enabling the reader to form a mental detailed picture of the actions in the stories.   He sometimes regarded them as mere vignettes that had flashed back swiftly from old memories retained in his head.   Yet this spontaneous power makes vivid the remarkable wonders of the magic nature between his lines.   His major concerns are with peasants, animals, with the land, and the order of nature.   He rarely tends to personify his animals but instead in his stories all mankind are animals, contrary to more conventional mainstream belief that human beings are the highest of all creatures on earth.   Men are not only a part of nature but are sometimes victims in the challenge of life and death when faced with the indifferent primitive force of the universe.

In the following chapters I intend to discuss some interesting aspects of his stories stemming from the literary techniques employed, such as the basic structure of his stories, style, diction and the nature and range of his varied stories.   From this I shall attempt to survey the beauty of his art in this celebrated genre rooted in the restless rebellious world of Liam O'Flaherty.

Chapter One:
Art of Storytelling

Cast a Cold Eye

Liam O'Flaherty's short stories fall into a very simple and conventional pattern. They follow the basic structure of a narrative with a starting point, a conflict which continues throughout the development of the plot in a certain form and follows the peak of the process, the climax, and a fast-paced ending without anti-climax. The author sometimes begins his stories at the point of conflict, the actions in the story being portrayed in a series of intense delineations, and then comes to an abrupt end.

His stories are short, without much detail in characterization, though he sometimes uses detailed and vivid description for visual effect. He does not explore in depth the psychological level of the characters, but represents the wonders of life in his stories. In contrast to the technique he uses for expressing the strengthened intensity of atmosphere or mood in his novels, which is always charged with melodrama and sentimentality, he employs in a simple direct depiction the elemental instincts of the characters in short stories (O'Brien 1973, 95-7).

The characters, humankind, animals or natural phenomena, portray the narrative directly. They appear as they are, full of rich imagery as in a picturesque vision without the complicated modern techniques of the experimental interior monologue, stream of consciousness or metaphor.   The speaking voice in the story is performed as the primary function of tale telling, not to impose overstatement or inflated symbolism, otherwise the author's overwhelming intrusion renders an inappropriate artless style which breaks down the oneness and the objectivity between the storyteller and his readers (Murray 157).   This detachment of the authorial intervention in the stories, expressed not explained, helps create O'Flaherty's finest vision of his literary world in short stories.

Liam O'Flaherty evokes an affinity, a communion, between the author's voice, the scene and his readers so that his stories operate in a pattern expressed in a vision of oneness (Washburn 120; Zneimer 158). His readers are in sympathy with the direct experiences that are expressed in the story as if they were present on the scene.   The boundaries between the author and his readers are blurred to reinforce the effect.

Liam O'Flaherty does not attempt to moralize or interpret the events he presents in those stories.   He works with "the style of omission," like Hemingway in his iceberg theory, for what is not said is more powerful (Washburn 120).   The author, being a component part of the complex life in nature, sees the manifestation of the grand motion of life without purpose to be symbolically embodied in a small creature, a wild flower, an insect or an animal (Zneimer 154-6). His performance in the form of writing is his means of reflecting the magic order of nature, which is beyond expression but with real significance, as in a looking glass.   The vision of his style is nature representing itself according to its law.   Liam O'Flaherty once described his style in one of his letters to Garnett as "a feeling of coldness," the extreme detachment, and with it the writer sees things possessing "a goat's eye" or "a snake's eye" (Zneimer 161).   Once the author's human qualities, such as sympathy and anguish, are brought into the vision, the objectivity of the style breaks down, and consequently pure artistry of this kind is then destroyed (Zneimer 161-3).

There are some examples of the adoption of the technique of objective narration in his stories.   Stories without human characters offer better examples of the quality, as sometimes human characters are easily moulded with a personality through their conversation, gestures and actions.   Admittedly, Liam O'Flaherty is occasionally so obsessed by what he is saying, that he intrudes, and imposes human terms on describing his animal characters.   These flaws can be found in stories like "The Wild Goat's Kid" (MS 10-5), "Jealous Hens" (MS 27-9) and "The Hook" (SS 70-2).

In "The Hook," for example, the author intrudes and interprets to say the seagull gets the bait liver "but he wanted to bring a share to his mate that was sitting on the eggs" (SS 70).   The other seagulls make a noise "blinking their eyes in amazement at the hook sticking from the trapped one's bill," and his mate on seeing the string cackles shrilly "like a virago of a woman reviling a neighbour" (SS 71-2; Zneimer 164).   The hens are portrayed as envious depressed concubines as they "watched, amazed and jealous" in "The Jealous Hens" (MS 28).   The black hen arranged her feathers beautifully, and she "fed assiduously and became so conceited and arrogant" (MS

29).   After the attack of those jealous hens, the black hen was not so beautiful as she was when she first arrived.   The cock "fussed about her, but it was plain that instead of feeling pity for her he was disgusted with her for being in such a disreputable condition" (MS 29).   Likewise the mongrel in "Two Dogs" (SS 67-9) is like a hero who eventually takes his revenge for the threat of losing territory to the greyhound.   In the above-mentioned instances the animals are presented as human characters, not to be described with a cold snake's eye.

Liam O'Flaherty, however, has depicted some fine sketches of his objects in the objective narration.   One good example is "The Wave" (SS 16-8) which has nothing like human or animal characters but depicts the vast mindless motion of ocean (Zneimer 161-3).   It is performed with O'Flaherty's photographic approach, as though to be presented as in a silent movie.   A similar pattern is employed in his masterpiece, "The Rockfish" (SS 29-31).   The "fundamental principles" are applied to display the order of nature with an ultimate detachment and objectivity from the observer (Zneimer 162).   No particular detailed description of the fisherman or the fish are present; he offers, instead, a series of events in its chronological order.   Cause and effect are not to be explained.   The tempo of the actions is fast-paced, and the story ends at its climax in one sentence: "He was free" (SS 31).   Other fine pieces such as "The Wild Swan" (WS 11-9), "Birth" (MS 73-6), "The Water Hen" (TL 64-8) and "The Fairy Goose" (MS 85-90) share in this quality: the author does not set himself up to interpret, to judge or explain in his own voice.

Double Masks

Born of a bilingual background, Liam O'Flaherty wrote mostly in English.   His collection of short stories <u>Dúil</u> (Desire), his only one in Irish, did not appear until as late as 1953.   Most of the Irish stories, had either been translated into English afterwards or, if translated from English, had their English counterparts.   Interestingly the two versions of the same story employed by these two different media of expression, English and Irish, are not wholly linguistically compatible with each other.   Murphy has commented that some of the Irish stories appear to be totally different stories from their English counterparts with different points of view, interpretation and verbal modification, so that they are to be shaped into a new form rather than a translation of the text (Murphy 1973, 21).

What motivated Liam O'Flaherty to put such double masks over his stories remains obscure.   It is amazing to discover how far these amendments were made by the author to show different atmospheres and colours within the narrative.   There appears to be a thematic divergence as well as a difference in style, characterization and tone (Murphy 1973, 21).

Some critics regard the Irish stories as superior to their English counterparts on the grounds that the language used in Irish versions is more lively, direct and terse, whereas it becomes artificial archaic, refined "bookish high-falutin" language in the English version (de Bhaldraithe 153).

The tone is more objective in the Irish stories.   In his famous story "The Cow's Death" (SS 13-5), the judgmental words *stupid* and *stupidly* are repeated in the text as "her *stupid* brain," "And then *stupidly* she pressed with her great bulk against the fence" and "She stood *stupidly* looking at it a long time, without moving a muscle" (SS 14-5).   There is no equivalent of such judgment in the Irish version "Bás na Bó," (DL 47-51, "The Cow's Death") which it describes how the cow with her maternal instinct shows her wonder and confusion about the missing calf and moves awkwardly but not *stupidly* (Murphy 1973, 24).

The style in "The Mouse" (TL 32-6) seems to be more artificial as he adds his interpretation to a natural image.   In "An Luchóg" (DL 108-114, "The Mouse") the scene that the kitten shakes his paws "díreach mar bheadh an talamh fliuch" (just as if the ground were wet; DL 113) becomes "to loosen the stricture of his muscle" in the English version (TL 35).[8]   And the description of the mouse escaping and moving on his belly as a snake ("Ar a bholg a chuaigh sé ar aghaidh, ar nós péiste"; DL 113-4) has been interpreted into the mouse's fear makes him to crawl on his belly (Murphy 1973, 24).

Liam O'Flaherty tends to stress the hard life of the island people while simultaneously showing their religious faith to his English readers. For example, there is no intrusive comments such as "poverty respects nothing" in "Daoine Bochta" (DL 85-90, "Poor People").   And in another story "Life" (TL 79-86) only the English version makes reference to poverty in the story (Murphy 1973, 22).   Besides he emphasizes religious piety in the English versions such as "An Buille" (DL 66-84, "The Blow") where the monologue in Irish "O!   A Thiarna Dia!   Nach orm a bhí an mí-ádh an lá a cuireadh faoi mo chúram do leithéid de phleidhce!" (Oh Lord God!   Didn't I have the bad luck the day he put this simpleton in my care; DL 69) turns out to be "Oh, God

Almighty!   This must be punishment for some unknown sin that I committed.   You have me crucified!   Crucified!" in English (SL 358; Murphy 1973, 23).   The tone is totally different.   Liam O'Flaherty even changes the characterization and atmosphere of the whole plot in another bilingual story "The Touch" (TL 54-63).

In the English version Liam O'Flaherty omits the cowardice of the young man, and makes the girl of the wealthy family, Kate, realize their predestined doomed love, then desperately give up and overcome her passion for the young man.   By contrast, in the Irish counterpart, "Teangabháil," Cáit ("Kate" in English) eventually rejects the young man because of his cowardice, which is also emphasized by the author in his repetition of the terms of "cowardice" or "coward" in relation to the young man in the story (DL 115-27).   Yet, this implication is not made at all in the English version (de Bhaldraithe 151-2).

The ambivalence existing in Liam O'Flaherty's stories in two languages, English and Irish, is paradoxical and complex.   He seems to rewrite his stories but provides a faithful translation for his readers. The two versions show distinct difference in tone, intention and intensity of power.   Apparently he attempts to create a filtered view of peasant's life on the Aran Islands for his English readers.   He may have done it for the purpose of publication, and acceptance by a wider readership in the English world (de Bhaldraithe 153).

The Visual and Aural Power of Words

Liam O'Flaherty is not highly praised for his manipulation of language; in fact, his style and diction are sometimes considered to be dull with too many repetitions and clichés. Some critics doubt his inheritance from the oral tradition as they do not regard his stories as good examples of that inheritance. The stories are designed to be for the visual image rather than the aural effect; that is, they are not very "oral."

Mercier once quoted Frank O'Connor's remarks on Liam O'Flaherty's language, to the effect that his English "lacks the distinction and beauty of his Gaelic."[9] He further argues that Liam O'Flaherty is the "least oral in his approach to narrative," if one compares his works to those of his contemporaries like Séan Ó Faoláin, and his animal stories are mostly conceived in "cinematic terms" (Mercier 1964, 105). Certainly, his stories on nature and animals are rich in imagery and are best performed in films. Reading through the pages, the delineation of the objects creates a vivid visual image on the brain.

Yet, he displays his powerful imagination in creating the atmosphere of the stories by using sound and rhythm. His prose has the poetic quality of tempo and rhyme as they are intended to be read aloud. A passage of the story "Wild Stallions" shows the lyrical qualities:

> Neighing hoarsely in his throat, the invader cantered forward slowly with his head bowed. The golden stallion stood his ground on widespread legs, mustering the last remnants of his strength, until the enemy swerved at close quarters to deliver a broadside. Then he rose and brought his forelegs down with great force. Struck above the kidneys, the grey uttered a shrill cry and fell. While rolling away, a second blow on the spine

made him groan and shudder from head to tail.   With his glazed
eyes wide open, he turned over on his back, swung his neck from
side to side and snapped his jaws without known purpose in the
urgent agony of death (PR 87) .[10]

His punctuation is designed to control the tempo and meaning of
words, as well as to draw readers' attention to the aural effect he has
created (Hampton 442).   Moreover, Liam O'Flaherty uses repetitive
images, symbols and expressions to strengthen the intensity of the
development of the plot and correlate them with the consciousness of his
characters for the sake of emphasis.   In some respects, his choice of
words is powerful and closely associated with the oral heritage which
still survives as Gaelic story-telling in the Aran Islands (Hampton 446).
There is one example to show the aural description is in the story
"The Letter" (MS 101-4).   It begins with a description of the
surroundings to establish the setting, serene and peaceful, under a clear
sky dotted with the gentle singing of larks.   The atmosphere is full of
joy and hope when the letter comes, reflecting the family's happiness for
the expected letter.   There follows the reading of the letter, the
speaking voice gradually changing to a low tone that tells the
heartbroken story of the girl.   The cheerful atmosphere switches to one
of looming sadness and gloom.   The continued singing of larks in the
closure is stark contrast to the despair and sorrow of the family.   There
is little dialogue in the story; the state of mind of characters is expressed
by the aural as well as the visual reference associated with their
surroundings.   Liam O'Flaherty sometimes uses body language such as
gestures, countenance and actions of characters to replace dialogue, in

order to show the inner state of mind of characters in the development of stories (Hampton 441).

The repetition of words, symbols and sentences marks his habitual technique of stressing motif, motivation or intensity of emotion in his characters.   For example, the word *crooning* appears four times at the beginning of the story "Milking Time" (SS 115-7): *"crooning* woman," "her *crooning* voice, red lips smiling as they *crooned"* and *"crooning* meaningless words of joy" (SS 115).   The word seems to be associated, symbolically, with maternal destiny of the woman (Hampton 443). The repetition of the sentences "Flow on, white water..." in "The Stream" (MS 108-11) entangles the old hag with her painful memories of a lost lover.   Repetition of archetypal symbols for birth, marriage and death is used to emphasize the motif in the stories like the lament in "Life" (TL 79-86), the repeated theme of marriage in "The Wedding" (TL 143-60) and death in "The Stream" (MS 108-111; Hampton 446).

There are also some repetitions which may be the result of the author's unconsciousness and carelessness such as the repetition of the monotonous word "something" in "The Landing" (SP 65-76) and a threefold repetition of "because" in "The Sinner" (MT 174-92), neither of which appears necessary for the sake of emphasizing or for special effect in the plot.   Notwithstanding, Liam O'Flaherty's mode of technique in this canon demonstrates his gift of visual imagination and the inheritance from the heritage of oral narration.

Chapter Two:
Motifs and Issues

Among many of his contemporaries, Liam O'Flaherty has been deemed to be one whose short stories present themselves with a realistic technique in a naturalistic climate. Some of his writings adopt an atmosphere of Darwin's determinism where only the fittest of the fittest will survive, where attention focuses on the cruel fate of living creatures, both human beings and animals, in the battlefield of survival [11]

His treatment of naturalism, however, is not so simple as to follow those naturalistic pioneers such as Jack London (1879-1916) who also depicts animal characters but as a kind of symbolic model for humans to emerge among peers; or Anton Chekhov (1860-1904) and Stephen Crane (1871-1900), whose characters are trapped and controlled by the predestined powerful social forces in their environment.

In this respect O'Flaherty's characters are not conspicuously controlled by the environment but mainly by their own weakness from the flaws of human nature. His stories are like mirrors reflecting the objects and facts in the universe, in order to "shame the devil."[12] Moreover, O'Flaherty's inclination towards naturalism appears ambivalent and complex, mixing the primitive zeal and passionate impulse as those shown in D. H. Lawrence's works.

Being castigated as an "inverted romantic" by Seán Ó Faoláin,[13] O'Flaherty delineates the major tragic destiny of people and animals, but primitive nature can also be their salvation and consolation.   O'Flaherty intends to represent the limitations and powerlessness of a tiny creature facing the awe and wonder of a grand mindless nature in the darkness of a chaotic universe of infinity.   The order of nature is so profound and powerful beyond human's control.

Since O'Flaherty was born and reared in a barren and remote primitive world, where he has experienced the ultimate beauty and miracle of nature as well as its indifference and its destructive power. The ambivalent force of nature, alternating between fertile and the destructive, seems mindless and apathetic, but it always maintains a virtual balance under a certain kind of nameless mysterious power. "Nature giveth and nature taketh away," and it truly sketches the harsh aspect of life on the Aran Islands (Cahalan 1991, 56).

Here again, O'Flaherty might not be confined to a conventional naturalistic writer on the grounds that his stories are not usually in an artificial setting, as in a big city.   In a conventional naturalistic view, people, especially those of lower class in a society, often have to face and accept their entrapped fate in an artificial hierarchical social mechanism controlled by a bureaucratic government.   People are always victims under such a system.

Yet, this belief of *predestination* is not O'Flaherty's major concern in his stories.   The disasters of his characters often result from the universal flaws of human nature regardless of their class or social positions-greed, jealousy, selfishness, possessiveness and inertia; their loss of innocence and failure to keep a harmonious relationship with their surroundings lead to their suffering or annihilation.   O'Flaherty's belief that the laws of nature are more akin to the oriental philosophy of Yin and Yang or deism, his admiring the grand power of the universe is obvious in his stories.[14]

An assessment of his corpus of stories reveals that the recurrent motif of praising energy and life force often takes the form of two opposing forces, or dual elements in the structure of his stories, and there are also representations of major themes such as struggle, tension, conflict, passion, life and death, which have all been played off against, or balanced with, each other.

Natural Laws: Determinism, Survival, Violence

Liam O'Flaherty expresses his own naturalistic point of view of primitive life in one of his autobiographies as follows:

> When a man is born on naked rocks like the Aran Islands, where the struggle for life against savage nature is very intense, the instinct for self-preservation is strong in him... life is an interminable process of one form of life preying on another, from the cow that destroys life in the blade of grass, to the lion that leaps upon a stag in the African forest.[15]

This passage from his book affords the reader an insight into his powered, yet simple, view of determinism, a view which he reiterates time and time again in his stories.   To O'Flaherty, the ceaseless cycle of birth and death, struggle and survival, is a stark feature in reality.   There is no concern for compassion or emotion in the games of the hunter and the prey.   The lion does not kill his prey just for pleasure but for survival, its basic instinct drives it to do so.   This may seem much too cruel and violent to people removed from harsh reality but O'Flaherty seems to instinctively sense that the whole ecosystem will keep a balance.[16]   Similarly, people exploit the more vulnerable animals, such as in husbandry and hunting, for their livelihood.

One of the most typically naturalistic stories in O'Flaherty's opus is "The Wounded Cormorant" (MS 30-32).   In this story, one of the cormorants' leg is accidentally broken by a loose rock, and afterwards the others attack the wounded one without mercy until it falls down into the sea.   Mercy and compassion do not exit when facing life and death. "The Wounded Cormorant" is not about O'Flaherty's treatment of mercy killing but about the nature law that only the fittest will survive in the light of Darwin's theory because they *really are* in reality.   In this piece, O'Flaherty depicts the occurrence with a technique of detachment but only in one sentence, inevitably he adds his own view to it: "But they had no mercy" (MS 32).

"The Rockfish" (SS 29-31) provides an alternative more fortunate example in this category of story.   Though the fish's flesh of its mouth has been torn by the hook, the fish survives to flee from the hand of the fisherman.   A similar outcome is apparent in "The Conger Eel" (MS 118-20), where the conger eel is caught along with a school of mackerel in a net by the fishermen in a boat at sea but is let go lest the conger eel would ruin their net.   But in O'Flaherty's stories, quite often survival is achieved at random and not by poetic justice according to an artificial phrase or judgment. This trait of detachment might be the most noticeable quality which differentiates O'Flaherty and other writers concerned with the animal kingdom. Though O'Flaherty writes some fablelike stories, his most memorable vignettes are usually performed with a cold, apathetic, photographic approach.

Two stories which illustrate this feature of his work are "The Oar" (MS 77-80) and "The Landing" (SS 32-7), in that both show the unpredictable fates of the fishermen on the island. The islanders have to depend on the sea to provide food and various other sources but sometimes the sea also devours their lives. In the "The Oar," for example, some people arrive ashore safely but some do not, whereas in "The Landing" the characters make strenuous efforts to land, and finally they succeed in doing so. In stories such as "The Black Rabbit" (MS 97-100), "Wild Stallions" (PR 80-8), "The Wild Goat's Kid" (MS 10-5) and "A Crow Fight" (PR 154-7), there is violent delineation of one creature preying on another, their competitive fight for survival.

In "Wild Stallions," for example, a golden stallion kills an invading rival but is wounded during the process and then is killed by mountain lions. "The Black Rabbit" is a story about a rabbit being killed by cats. But in this story, the animals have a human personality imposed upon them. The rabbit is intelligent and cunning like "the first monkey that became inspired with the vision of humanity" (MS 98). For some mysterious, unspoken reason, the housekeeper "on the point of swooning with fright and shame," takes a superstitious dislike to the rabbit who has grown so large and cunning, and the housekeeper reverts to spitefully swearing "by the Holy Book" (MS 99). A bloody scene ensues at the end of the story when a troop of cats *in revenge* arrive and then tear the rabbit into pieces.   This story, however, seems to be too artificial instead of being objective and natural.   In "A Crow Fight," the fighting is started by a mother crow in order to get a new nest for her young to replace the one she has just lost.   In such stories, no moral lesson seems to emerge and the representation of the violent, conflicting nature of life seems to be the sole objective.   As Thompson asserts, they are "celebrations of the workings of instinct and appetite, of the biological chain, and of the struggle of natural selection which often brings random death to living creatures but never dishonor" (81).

Life Force, Courage, Rebelliousness and Energy

Scanning through the spectrum of O'Flaherty's stories, one is struck by the fact that there are a number of them affirming life, impulse, energy, even violence and passion, especially in sexuality, instead of stressing pessimistic determinism and death.   Although death is the eventual lot of many of his characters, they are, nevertheless, admirably praised by O'Flaherty for their primitive, courageous energy with Promethean attributes in his stories (Thompson 81).   In many respects violence is the hallmark of O'Flaherty's novels and this same quality can be seen to dominate in his stories except that here seems to be a different point of view and approach adopted.   Violence, in other words, is also a mode of expression of energy and rebelliousness, both of which are the essence of life to O'Flaherty.   His splendid ferocity in writing and in personality has announced itself in one of his numerous contributions to The Irish Statesman:

But the human race has not advanced from savagery to culture on the feeble crutches of philosophy... Let us not be ashamed that gunshots are heard in our streets.   Let us rather be glad.   For force is, after all, the opposite of sluggishness.   It is an intensity of movement, of motion.   And motion is the opposite of death.[17]

O'Flaherty's *call of the wild* manifests his basic belief in the patterns he uses to weave some of his short stories.   The motion, either in the form of ferocious frenzy, verging on the violent, or insanity has been shown in the development of a conflict, a fighting or a struggle in stories.   Representatives of this type are exemplified by the energetic life force in "The Wild Goat's Kid" (MS 10-5), the courage in "The Foolish Butterfly" (MS 1-9) and the passion in "The Caress" (PR 196-222) and "Josephine" (TL 224-36) and "The Mermaid" (PR 89-95).

The celebration of energy and life impulse marks the intense feeling in "The Wild Goat's Kid" (MS 10-15).   A goat wanders away from her master's house, and starts her own life in a wild world.   After the birth of her defenseless kid, she is compelled to defeat and kill a marauding dog.   This story is full of O'Flaherty's fast-paced motion and activity, full of fury and primitive drive.   The passage describing the goat urging her kid to rise shows the intensity of energy and instinct to survive, which are the thematic points in the story:

Then he stood up, trembling, staggering, swaying on his curiously long legs.   She became very excited, rushing around

> him, bleating nervously, afraid that he should fall again.   He fell.
> She was in agony.   Bitter wails came from her distended jaws
> and she crunched her teeth.   But she renewed her efforts, urging
> the kid to rise, to rise and live...to live, live, live. (MS 11)

The threefold repetition of the word "live" affirms the author's major concern of "energy" and "force" in life, and that is also his greatest admiration for the wild creatures in his deepest passion (Kennelly 183).

A celebration of courage is portrayed in "The Foolish Butterfly" (MS 7-9), in which a butterfly flies out to sea, and after a while the frail creature runs out of energy and gets lost.   Finally it falls into water and drowns.   The author describes the beauty as well as innocence of the little butterfly as a "godly thing" (MS 7).   Its adventure out on the sea is a process of learning, trying to survive in an indifferent world. Though the story ends in death, the courageous try is mostly extoled by the author.   O'Flaherty's concern is not about success or failure but the noble spirit of courage and endurance.   The butterfly may be ignorant, but there is no implied regret in O'Flaherty's description of the way nature works: "There were a few little movements of the round head. Then the butterfly lay still" (MS 9; Thompson 81).

In some of these stories, the mode of energy transforms into passion, especially sexuality such as "The Caress" and "Josephine." "The Caress," for instance, the girl Mary and her lover Martin lay on the open grass, and "their cries of love rose into the night like prayers of thanksgiving and of triumph of the divine source of life" (PR 216). O'Flaherty connects sexuality with religious reference; the "divine source of life" originates from primitive passion. At the end of the story, Mary and Martin plan to elope to America for a new life. Though their adventure is so unpredictable, these two young hearts are full of hope. Unlike some of the characters portrayed in O'Flaherty's urban stories, where the characters are spiritually dead due to their ageing condition in their timidity and dull, numbed condition. Here, O'Flaherty's manifestation of acclaimed energetic life force is found in passion and sexuality.

Duality and Dichotomy

Liam O'Flaherty uses dual imagery as opposing forces to intensify the powerful feelings in his stories. The dual complexity, co-existence of a peaceful calm atmosphere in contradistinction to a frenzied ferocity, joy as opposed to sorrow, youth to old age, life to death, sterile to fertile are largely found in his stories. The duality, expressed more often as a dichotomy, intensifies the motif of conflict in the narrative.

Liam O'Flaherty's view of Aran, perhaps a microcosm of a prototype world, is one encompassing dual opposing forces. It may not be difficult to note that Liam O'Flaherty comes from such a place with terrible beauty of landscape, Pagan-Christian mixed culture, innocence mixed with ignorance and superstitions, all manifest in his stories. O'Flaherty himself also embodies this aspect duality and dichotomy by his inconsistency and self-contradiction in beliefs, behavior as well as in his writings. The ambivalence of life and death can be seen in "Life" (TL 79-86), youth and old age in "The Stream" (MS 108-11) and "The Wedding" (TL 143-60); rise and fall in "Two Lovely Beasts" (TL 7-31) and "The Eviction" (TL 171-82); and sterility and fertility in "Red Barbara" (MS 122-28) and "The Wedding."

In "Life," the ambivalence lies in the contrast condition of the new born grandson and the dying grandfather.   As the joy of a new child is abounds within the family, the decay of an elderly man is accelerating. The old man dies soon after the birth of the baby.   It is a cycle of life and death that a new one seems to come in the place of the other.   The stark contrast of the strong new life and the decay of old age is given here: the "strong young heart was unaware that the tired old heart had just delivered up the life that made it beat" (TL 86).

This dual senses of rise and fall also run through a similar pattern in the stories "Two Lovely Beasts" and "The Eviction."   Similarly, in the story "Two Lovely Beasts," the emergence (or the birth) of one prosperous family, the Colms, is juxtaposed with the misfortune of the widow Kate Higgins and her family, which causes her death and the hardship of her family eventually, the destruction of another family.   In O'Flaherty's socialist view of the capitalized society, the selfish capitalists are to be condemned as blood-suckers, such as Colm in this case.   The author's judgment is made by one of the characters, Gorum, that it's "too wild and barren here for any one man to stand alone. Whoever tries to stand alone and work only for his own profit becomes an enemy of all" (TL 17).   Yet, reality often reflects the converse, begging the author's question: "if what he is doing is bad, why does he prosper?" (TL 22)   O'Flaherty tries to justify his socialist belief by means of Gorum's predicted remarks that, "... The time will soon come, though, when the bloodsuckers that are robbing us will be struck down by the hand of Almighty God.   They will roast in Hell for the everlasting ages" (TL 31).   Still, O'Flaherty's apocalyptic ending is treated in a paradoxical complexity.

The duality of youth and old age is present in "The Stream" (MS 108-11) and The Wedding (TL 143-60).   The story starts with a contrast between a contented young woman and a witchlike crone who is portrayed as ugly and evil in the description of her awkward physical appearance and her sound "like the death rattle in a dying man's throat" (MS 109).   The sharp contrast of youth and old age is made again in retrospect of the old hag's story sixty years ago; her young, pretty image in the past in contrast with her old, ugly and evil-looking at present.   The stream witnesses the old hag's whole story, her heartbreaking memories and the withered insanity in her current life.

In "Red Barbara," the ambivalence and dichotomy in sterility and fertility are obvious in the theme of the story.   They are also used to stress the powerlessness of the well-educated Joseph and the wild nature of Barbara.   The story is about a conflict between two forces, refined, suppressed culture from human society versus wild, primitive power from nature, embodied by Joseph and Barbara. O'Flaherty gives his own poetic justice in the story, where the artificial, cultured man Joseph is defeated by the naive, wild Barbara, which also justifies Barbara's identity as daughter of the people. The pale, sluggish artificialities are shown in Joseph's *modesty*, *tenderness* and also sterility.   On the contrary, the primitive sexuality of Barbara and the fishermen ensures the survival of the species, fertility (O'Connor 1972, 51).

Evil, Weakness and Powerlessness

Life is frail and tiny in an infinite universe.   In O'Flaherty's stories
human beings, due to their physical and intellectual limitations, are
always exposed by their weakness and powerlessness in human nature,
which sometimes lead to their downfall, in O'Flaherty's stories.
Animals, rather than mankind, seem to appear more akin to ideal beauty
in O'Flaherty's world.   Intellect distinguishes mankind and animals but
the complexity of human intelligence also causes evil and annihilation
in some of O'Flaherty's stories such as "The Stone" (MS 117-21),
"Blood Lust" ((TL 99-103), "The Pedlar's Revenge" (PR 17-33) and "A
Pot of Gold" (SS 76-81).

Human pride is the tragic flaw of the character in the story "The
Stone."   The old man, once the strongest one in the village, tries to
make his efforts to lift the stone high as he used to do in his youth.[18]
Yet, the reminiscence of youth kills him because strength has been on
the wane as time goes by.   His failure to see his own physical
limitations at age results in his destruction at the end.   The author's
main point makes clear: "There is nothing in all creation that isn't more
lasting than man" (MS 121).   Yet again, the Gaelic influence is felt
here as this is a translation of the Gaelic phrase "Is beag rud nach buaine
é náon duine."

The evil of jealousy is portrayed in "Blood Lust."   Two brothers
are fishing together on a boat at sea.   The protagonist's lack of
confidence and jealousy motivates him to kill his brother, nevertheless,
his cowardice and hesitation drive him to fulfill his blood lust by
crushing a fish he just caught.   His evil notion toward his brother does

not result from his brother's inadequate deeds or wrongdoing but is somehow deeply rooted in the original sin of human beings. But the protagonist fails to realize that his deed might cost his life as well, if a fight results, especially on a boat.

In "The Pedlar's Revenge," hatred and obsession of revenge entangle the Pedlar until his lifelong enemy is dead. Partly being mixed with comic atmosphere, the story also displays the rooted evil of malice in human nature. Human greed and foolishness are expressed in the story "A Pot of Gold" in a comic way. A man tells his villagers that he has had a dream about a pot of gold which in fact, does not exist at all. A group of people start out to search for the clues allegedly seen in the dream vision. Finally the villagers discover it is a trick, but dare not do anything in revenge or their foolishness, which is driven by their greed would be known. These two pieces are treated with a comic style, showing people's obsessions may lead to chaos, disorder and delusion.

Another example of revenge is in the story "The Black Mare" (SS 55-9), where the protagonist owns a good horse and treats her with love and care. But when in a horse race, he strikes his mare a heavy blow in order to win favor with a girl spectator. His mare becomes insensed at that, and then races at wreckless speed towards a rock. The protagonist gets a broken leg as well as losing a fine horse and good companion.

People are portrayed powerless when facing life and death in O'Flaherty's stories. The sense of loneliness and isolation is found at the moment of birth and death such as the old man in "Galway Bay" (TL 218-21; O'Connor 1972, 48). He walks his old cow to the fair to sell her to pay for his funeral. He feels isolated from his family because he is left alone to face death at the end.   "Going into Exile" (SS 98-107) conveys the loneliness of people at the moment of departure.   It might be the family's last meeting in their life.   The young people have to leave for America to make a living.   Thus the inevitable sorrow of departing from one's family also shows people's powerlessness in life.[19]

Chapter Three:
Spectrum of Short Narratives

Liam O'Flaherty's short fiction creates a wide spectrum of experience. He wrote about people and animals in a remote wild world, his fictitious Aran, in most of his short stories. Their struggle and survival instincts are portrayed in a simple, sometimes dull and flat, style.

The motifs of the profound mindless power and the everlasting cycle of nature manifest themselves in the lives of these creatures. Rarely romantic, Liam O'Flaherty did write something about love and the relationship between sexes, but with a more realistic, sometimes naturalistic, tone. To the people and animals in such a barren island, life is cruelly harsh and non-romantic in reality. It is rarely full of joy and laughter, but more often it portrays hardship and suffering. There is always birth juxtaposing with death, success with failure, rise with fall in a real world.

Liam O'Flaherty consciously or sub-consciously manipulates his "politics" between the lines. The consciousness of conveying some "ideas" in the text appears on the surface of the plot in some of his stories, which are often criticized as "artificial" and "overly obvious in theme, and flat in effect" with less force and beauty by some critics (Doyle 1971, 115). Many of his stories are vignettes of country scenes and wildlife with a poetic "intensity and strong momentum" (Kennelly 175).   The varied types of O'Flaherty's stories include parables, fables, legends, satire, comedy, stories about love and relationship, and ecological pieces.

Parables, Fables and Dreamy Legends

Once having been remarked as "a dreamy poet" as well as "a sarcastic realist" by A. A. Kelly in her introduction to a reprint of Liam O'Flaherty's short story collection The Pedlar's Revenge (1996), Liam O'Flaherty wrote several pieces from the basis of a Christian-Pagan myth in Aran where superstitions and legends still pervade (12-3). Actually many of his stories are parablelike that seem to touch on perpetual matters in life and life itself.   The examples are stories like "Spring Sowing" (SS 7-12), "The Fairy Goose" (MS 85-90), "Two Lovely Beasts" (TL 7-31), "The Mermaid" (PR 89-95) and "The Salted Goat" (PR 119-124), the last two of which collected in a late story collection   The Pedlar's Revenge (1976) seem to draw less attention to literary critics than the others.

"Spring Sowing" is a parable of human destiny--combination of human duties, joy and sorrows, young and old, birth and death (Doyle 1971, 46).   The newly-wedded couple Martin and Mary perform the "time-honoured ritual with notable enthusiasm and even holiness" in participating in their first sowing since their marriage (Doyle 1971, 46). They enjoy their work done together because they are still under the bloom of their fresh love.   Martin makes efforts to "prove himself a man worthy of being the head of a family by doing his spring sowing well" (SS 7).   It is a ritual of adulthood for him and Mary as well.   He says to his wife Mary that, "... it's no boasting to say that ye might well be proud of being the wife of Martin Delaney... You did your share better than any woman in Inverara could in this blessed day" (SS 12). This suggests Mary's everlasting household duties as being a farmer's wife; the spring sowing also, symbolically, refers to her future maternal destiny (Doyle 1971, 47).

The ritual of sowing for the young couple symbolizes the same fundamental in all marriage and family life, and Martin and Mary have to accomplish their task year after year until they are aged, when new love and labour will turn out to be routine and monotonous, until the day their younger generations are to take over the task in the future.   Their first day is the microcosm of their whole life.   They realize that their task, in communion with nature, of performing an act "not only vital, but, to some degree, mystic and holy" (Doyle 1971, 47).   The essence of this story is representative of O'Flaherty, the perpetual ritual of planting and reaping, or in Vivian Mercier's phrase, the portrayal of a character "as the celebrant of timeless mysteries--mysteries rooted in Nature and in that portion of Nature embodied in the life of Man."[20]

"The Fairy Goose" is a religious fable of mixing Pagan-Christian myth with reality.   A literary critic James H. O'Brien suggests it is a simple piece which utilizes "the simple permanent world of peasants to dramatize a cycle of a religious belief," the rise and fall of a myth in a community, like a kind of history of religion (O'Brien 1973, 114). "The Fairy Goose" tells the story of a gosling who is believed to have magic power but later the myth is destroyed by a priest, whose deed also contributes to the death of the goose at the end of the story.   In the aftermath of the death of the fairy goose, the villagers become quarrelsome drunkards.

This story seems to imply an ironic moral lesson, criticizing the suppression or the opposition, under the guise of righteousness, from the Church.   This story reminds one of an ancient Chinese myth, the legend of White Snake, in which the white snake is expelled from her house and gaoled in a pagoda by a monk.[21]   The fairy goose, like the white snake, is harmless to people.   Yet in the history of a religion, especially in a monotheistic world, the conformity of a religious belief often causes the persecution of the alternative.   "The Fairy Goose" shows the perverse ingenuity, ignorance and cruelty of man, a "degeneration once a myth has been removed," and a "nostalgia" for the good old days (O'Brien 1973, 114).

"The Salted Goat" is another fablelike story, which tells a story about an eccentric old man called Patsy preserving his beloved goat, Peg, who is his sole companion after his wife's death, in order to keep her spirit in his house by salting her in a tub.   Eventually he died of hunger as he insists on his idea of keeping his "goat" in his house and refuses to leave the house lest "the fairy will fly away with Peg" (PR 123).   At the end of the story people believed that "the goat was a devil and that Patsy had sold himself to her" (PR 124).

There are some references associated the goat with evil spirit in the story such as the description of the goat's peculiar yellow eyes, the neighbour's habit of making the sign of the cross and two other unusual happenings that preceded the death of the goat (PR 121).   But actually Patsy does not appear to be a Faust-like figure having a bargain with devil, and the author does not describe Patsy in a negative sense.   His peculiar action of skinning and salting the goat just in order to keep her "spirit" because he adores the goat as a surrogate wife.

Instead Patsy is portrayed as a "saintly innocent," figure which can be explained by the description of the birds feeding from his hand offering an image of St. Francis (Murphy 1979, 60). He may be peculiar or insane to the commoners but he is harmless; his insanity "was more akin to that of the ancient hermits who clothed themselves in sackcloth and ashes and went to live in a desert among wild beasts and birds" (PR 121). Patsy's ritual might be viewed as a saint's legend associated with St. Patrick, "Saint Resuscitates Pagan's Bull," who is skinned and salted but later is miraculously restored by St. Patrick as a demonstration of faith. Patsy's vigil lies in his witness, his starvation and his sacrifice for his ideal; and to those simple-minded villagers, something mysterious may be malevolent to them (Murphy 1979, 60-1).

"The Mermaid" is a mystical legend. It tells of a sad love story. The angelic young man McNamara turns against God for the loss of his love, Margaret. The atmosphere of the whole story is portrayed as in a dream vision. The sublime beauty is too frail to survive in a mortal world. The howling storm is believed to be the mermaid's singing at night in a folk belief. Some islanders who never come back from fishing are believed to have been seduced and taken away by mermaids at sea. It is also interesting to note that another "coastal" aspect of O'Flaherty's writing that of the mermaid, features prominently in the work of contemporary Gaelic poet Nuala Ní Dhomhnaill (1952-), and both authors have clearly drawn on Gaelic folklore and folk belief. People's superstition is shown in a sentence about the death of a beauty in the story that, "the God Crom had taken her for his bride" (PR 93).   The rural peasants tend to have their own explanations for the natural phenomenon or anything unknown and mysterious to them.   Some other stories such as "Beauty" is employed in an Edenic myth of snake and tree, manipulating the archetype of seduction (SP 77-81).   "Sport: The Kill" (SS 60-2) is a story about a boy and his dog cruelly hunting and killing a rabbit.   It may be observed as a parody of the hunting game in the adult's world, moreover, the hunting formula in a war.

Lyrical Vignettes

A large number of Liam O'Flaherty's stories may be considered lyrical vignettes of country scenes and life.   Some are even free of human or animal characters such as the story "The Wave" (SS 16-8).   In this story, O'Flaherty describes a cliff at high tide in the story.   The waves meet midway and crash against the cliff, come soaring into the cove from two reefs.   A giant wave gathers far out in the cove, being described as a magnificent animate creation, which manifests the author's admiration for the great destructive force (O'Connor 1972, 54).   "For a moment the wave stood motionless, beautifully wild and immense" (SS 17).   This treatment of the wave crashing to the shore is also a feature of the work of the Donegal author Seosamh Mac Grianna (1901-1990) in the opening portion of his novel An Druma Mór (The Big Drum, 1969).   Here again, we see O'Flaherty's ability to personify the inanimate, such as the wave, or evoke sympathy for creatures normally associated with emotions of pain and fear such as goldfish in a crystal bowl.

Some stories are descriptive accounts of a moment of conflict or tension such as "The Rockfish" (SS 29-31) and "The Blackbird" (SS 38-40).   "The Rockfish" is a story about a fish being almost caught. There is someone fishing at the sea.   A huge rockfish emerges from his lair and gulps the baited hook.   He is dragged nearly into the fisherman's hand.   The struggle continues on for a while.   The top hook breaks and the line jerks up.   The rockfish tries to breathe with open mouth, and he hurls himself into the air and dives downwards violently.   And suddenly the hook tears a strip of skin out of his jaw. He escapes eventually.

"The Blackbird" is about a cat approaching a blackbird from behind in order to catch it.   The blackbird does not realize his danger but keeps on singing alone in the darkness until a gust of wind strikes him sideways, and he finds out that he is "making fool of himself singing out there in complete darkness... he (is) filled with disgust" (SS 40).   The cat's claw just lands on his tail the moment when he is flying away.   He is fortunate in that the cat does not actually catch him but his little heart is, nevertheless, panting with fright.   The above-mentioned pieces are prime examples of O'Flaherty's keen observations of wildlife, which often deal with the theme of the hunter and the hunted.   The setting and characterization are less important and even neglected aspects, because the author's principal focus is on the action in such stories. It seems to be timeless and universal.   Frank O'Connor once claimed that his animal stories are the "masterly presentations of instinctual life" and in many ways the same claim could be made for the short stories of Liam O'Flaherty.[22]

The stories like "Milking Time" (SS 115-7), "Three Lambs" (SS 47-50), "Birth" (MS 73-6), "The Oar" (MS 77-80), "Galway Bay" (TL 208-221) and "Life" (TL 79-86) are about the lives of peasants, the everyday matters and everlasting cycle of life and death. The stories which focus, in particular, on the hardship of poor people's lives are ones like "Poor People" (MS 33-5), "The Letter" (MS 101-4), "The White Bitch" (PR 125-8) and Galway Bay (TL 209-21).

"The White Bitch," for example, tells a story that a couple have to drown their pet dog because they have no money for the dog license. O'Flaherty uses a more soft and emotional tone, delineating the poor people's self-contradictory state of mind and hesitation of *doing or not doing* in this story. Without enough money, they cannot even keep their beloved dog. The story ends with a romantic atmosphere in which the couple change their mind to retrieve her. The author does not attempt to tell us what the couple plan to do to pay for the license afterwards, but merely paints readers a picture of a happy ending that "(h)e pulls her up into the boat and caresses her in his arms lovingly" (PR 128).   This is not a usual formula of O'Flaherty's stories as most of the time the storyteller narrates his stories in a more realistic and naturalistic tone.

Another story "Poor People" can be interpreted as a typical O'Flaherty's story concerning the miserable lot of poor people. A poor couple whose little boy is very ill and confined to his bed eventually lose him at the end of the story. O'Flaherty creates a low tone in his delineation of physical weakness and weariness of the man Derrane and a gloomy air of sadness looms over the whole story "he remembered the sadness that awaited him there, lamentation and a grave being opened..." (MS 34).

But his stories are by no means always sad ones.   The pieces such as "Three Lambs," "Milking Time" and "Birth," are full of joy and wonder.   "Birth" can be viewed as a parallel story of the sad story about maternity "The Cow's Death" (SS 13-5), only that this time the author gives a remarkable picture of the pain of labour and the joy of birth.   In stories such as these, events seem to have been trawled straight from the author's memories in that O'Flaherty provides first-hand observation for his readers in the stories.

Satire, Comedy and Trick Stories

Liam O'Flaherty's anti-clerical attitude is frequently expressed in some of his satirical stories concerning clergymen.   To O'Flaherty the priests are like greedy politicians and are often depicted as bad and corrupt in his stories (Cahalan 1991, 37).   This animosity towards the clergy is understandable if one recalls O'Flaherty's early childhood experience of a boycott of his family instigated and led by a parish priest. O'Flaherty once wrote a satiric chapter on priests in a booklet that, "The parish priest has a finger in every pie.   He is the great and only power in the district."[23]   Furthermore he remarked, "I never could see any difference between a man being a pimp and being pope."[24]   The stories describing priests in a negative sense are pieces like "Offerings" (MS 24-6), "The Outcast" (TT 181-8) and also "The Fairy Goose" (MS 85-90).

In "Offerings" the priest is portrayed as a greedy man who pockets the money that people bring to the wake for Paddy Lenehan's four-year-old daughter.   Apparently in the story the priest does not concentrate on reading and praying but spends his time watching or peeping at the money.   The notorious priests in "The Fairy Goose" and "The Outcast" are harsh and cold.   In both stories the priests are held responsible for the respective destruction and death of the goose and the young woman.   The goose in "The Fairy Goose" and the young woman in "The Outcast" are employed in a similar pattern in that they are both frail and harmless, especially the woman who is in desperate state of helplessness.   The priests appear as villains to strike and banish Mary Wiggins, the owner of the fairy goose, and the goose herself.   Eventually the village becomes a cursed place of quarrelsome drunkards who "fear God but do not love one another" (MS 90).

In "The Outcast" the priest's harsh rejection of the helpless young unmarried woman who has just had a baby causes her to commit suicide with her baby.   Without Christian love, the priests are portrayed as persecutors on the pretext of righteousness.   Likewise, the priest in the story "Mackerel for Sale" (MT 115-31) is portrayed as a hypocrite, an impotent organ in the mechanism of a society.   In O'Flaherty's perception, the Church is too rich while the people are too poor in Ireland.   The priests preach to people but do not feel impelled to do anything to improve the society.   In many of O'Flaherty's stories, the severe attack on priests is obvious, and in many cases excessive religious piety is "literary against nature" in O'Flaherty's world (Gonzalez 89).

Liam O'Flaherty's socialistic empathy with the lower class is also shown to make the lower class play tricks on or triumph over the higher, usually middle class, in some of what might be termed his trick stories.   Some trick stories also demonstrate the foolishness and obsessions of people in a comic way.   Examples of such trick stories are, "A Red Petticoat" (MS 39-45), "Colic" (SP 215-23), "A Pot of Gold" (SS 76-81), "Pedlar's Revenge" (PR 17-33), "The Sensualist" (TT 237-50), "The Old Hunter" (MS 16-23), "The Stolen Ass" (MS 55-7) and "Unclean" (WS 41-60).

"Colic" tells a story that two people play tricks on the owner of the public house in order to obtain a drink for nothing.   "A Red Petticoat" is a also story about a trick on a shopkeeper.   A poor woman earns her credit for her groceries from the shopkeeper because she knows about the shopkeeper's secret affair with a tailor.   The same pattern of the lower class outwitting over the higher class appears again in the story "Unclean."   It is about a prostitute who deceives a man and tricks him out of his money, which makes the man become a dupe in the slum.   In "The Stolen Ass" a peasant attempts to talk his way around the facts about his theft of the ass.   The author creates humorous atmosphere of the story concerning the word play and language.

Stories on Relationships between Men and Women

As has been stated at the beginning of this chapter, Liam O'Flaherty did not write many stories about love and relationship between men and women.   He is often classified as a misogynist due to his ill treatment and sexual stereotyping of women in some of his stories (Cahalan 1991, 41).   But sometimes the author's voice seems to be with the weaker role of women.   His dual attitude toward the gender roles remains ambivalent and inconsistent in his stories on men and women. Examples are like "The Touch" (TL 54-63), "The Caress" (PR 196-222), "Red Barbara" (MS 122-8), "The Stream" (MS 108-111), "The Ditch" (MT 49-56) and "Josephine" (SP 224-36).

A few of O'Flaherty's stories portray a picture of young women as victims of a patriarchal marriage-market in a conservative community (Cahalan 1991, 47).   "The Touch" is a good example.   It is a story about the doomed love between a rich girl and a poor young man.   The girl Kate has to marry another older neighbour instead of the one she desires, Brian, by her father's arrangement.   Their doomed love is predestined for the difference between their classes.   Kate's father shouts to the young man, "A cat can look at a princess... It's a different story, though, when a blackguard that doesn't have a penny to his name looks at a decent man's daughter" (TL 57).   That explains all.   Kate feels herself being treated as commodity sold on a market, the marriage market, and that is her fate.   Indeed women are often treated in a similar degrading fashion in such a conservative community.   The future career for a woman always refers to her marriage.

"Josephine" is, however, a story opposite to "The Touch," in that the protagonist Josephine chooses to marry a man, she does not love, for money.   It was a very common occurrence for a poor girl to do it just that in order to be rid of poverty.   In this story, the young woman Josephine is a more calculating and clever character, and in one sense, at least, she is able to make her own choice for her future.

In Another story "Red Barbara," the protagonist is a strong woman, an unusual type of woman in O'Flaherty's stories. The author furthermore accentuates the stark contrast between the strong Barbara and her weak weaver husband Joseph in the narrative. Barbara even *refuses* to be conceived by Joseph, which is a disgrace for a husband. Barbara remains childless until she marries the third time after the death of Joseph.

O'Flaherty's stories on dealing with men and women normally emphasize the key role of passion between sexes, suggesting that they are best occupied copulating and producing children, as reflected from Aran animal life in the mating season (Cahalan 1991, 46). The essential example is like a mating competition in "The Water Hen" (TL 64-8) or in "The Wild Swan" (WS 11-9), violent and passionate; after his (the cock's) victory in a fight over a water hen, "in a moment he was upon her and she lay down in a swoon" (TL 68).

Stories of Ecological Conscience

Some attention from literary critics has been drawn to O'Flaherty's short stories about his ecological concern. His affinity for "pastoralism" and animal fables prove him to be one of the modern writers to demonstrate an ecological awareness and sensitivity. His major consciousness of the relationship between the earth and its inhabitants evokes a vision rendering his wish for a harmonious united world (Scher 114).

O'Flaherty places those imbued with the traits of innocence and primitive impulse higher in the hierarchy of his literary world as opposed to his loathing for the educated civilized men.   In such a world, the survival instinct is the chief biological drive, the force of life.   Men and animals are subject to these powerful drives in order to ensure survival (O'Connor 1972, 47).   Likewise O'Flaherty suggests that man's tolerance for the lower species should be based on more than "utility" in his stories (O'Connor 1972, 53).

The story "Milking Time" (SS 115-7) demonstrates the quality of being in harmony with the earth and other species: the emotional air of a happy man and his wife and their cow.   They share a symbiosis with each other.   This is a prototype of O'Flaherty's ecological conscience in his short stories.

"The Cow's Death" (SS 13-5), on the contrary, shows not the stupidity of the cow but rather the stupidity of people, for the death of a cow is a big loss for a peasant family (Scher 119).   The same pattern appears in "The Wild Sow" (SS 73-5), in which the hunger-struck sow eats up Neddy's stored food and finally dies with a potato choked in her throat.   At first Neddy feeds her, and later he deserts and keeps her out of his cabin.   The wild sow's hunger, her basic instinct for survival, drives her to search for food.   The death of the sow, which is a big loss to him, results from his irresponsibility and stupidity.   He believes that keeping a pig is like having money in the bank.   But at the end all he has but a stone dead body.   He has nothing left.

To O'Flaherty, animals and innocents, such as children, are more close to the ideal beauty in his world because they share an ecological innocence in harmony with nature, the earth.   People tend to lose the same quality of innocence partly due to "the process of acculturation" (Scher 115). "Three Lambs" (SS 47-50) is such a story about an ideal integrated relationship between human beings and the natural cycle of the earth. Little Michael gets up early to watch the black sheep's lambing. He becomes more like a gentle and helpful assistant than a mere observer during the lambing. The *three* lambs are foreshadowed by the earlier mention of a prize of *three* pancakes offered for the first one who sees the lamb in the story (Scher 118). This fresh experience of watching the process of birth appears an enlightenment for the child, exposing himself to the ewe and wonder of nature and from it little Michael can further sympathies with the same pain of childbirth his own mother endured.

Urban Stories

In many of O'Flaherty's short stories, the setting is often found in a rural area, dealing with the vitality of peasants' hard lives. In some of his stories which take place in an urban setting, however, the characters always appear sluggish, numb or spiritually paralyzed. Like some of Séan O'Faoláin's works or many of James Joyce's stories in Dubliners (1914), the urban stories are about the characters' misplaced illusion in a disillusioned modern Ireland, or their internal spiritual condition reflected on a tangible external correlation between setting and characters.[25] The quest for a simple country life in those urban stories seems to be a means of "rejuvenation" and revival from a suffocating state of spiritual paralysis like many characters in O'Flaherty's novels (Gonzalez 85).

The atmosphere of paralysis in the urban stories is created by means of establishing a setting as a claustrophobic limited space, the characters' ageing and conservative attitudes in cowardice, sluggishness and lack of innocence which renders meanness, hypocrisy and distrust. The settings are often in a limited-spaced enclosure such as a stuffy room where Joseph Timmins sits with his wife in "The Fall of Joseph Timmins" (MT 132-49); a shadowy, gloomy yard of a workhouse hospital in "The Tramp" (SS 19-28).

The lack of youthful vitality suggests the characters' ageing. In "The Fall of Joseph Timmins" the protagonist Joseph is fifty years old; the aging of Deignan is shown in "The Tramp" and the suggested old age of the villagers in "Mackerel for Sale" is depicted by their "timidity, closed-mindedness and extreme self-righteousness" (Gonzalez 87). Again, there is always a juxtaposition of another character, youthful, vibrant and vigorous, in contrast with the paralyzed numb character in the stories. The tramp is a vulgar man to the civilized educated Deignan but is also one who enjoys a vital and carefree life in "The Tramp." The tramp's way of life is appealing to Deignan, but he does not have the courage to change his current lifestyle, though sluggish and dull, and to give up his notions of *civility* and *respectability*. He regards that living in a papers' hostel is still higher than that of being a tramp (Doyle 50).

Joseph is starkly contrasted with his young nephew Reggie in "The Fall of Joseph Timmins" and the animated character Bartly Tight in "Mackerel for Sale." The vital characters appear to be "potential saviours," suggest "a means of escape or of renewal" because these urban stories mainly deal with the death of the living spirit, or soul, of these people (Gonzalez 89).   Again, the urban people's snobbery and hypocrisy are portrayed much more in these stories, also showing O'Flaherty's cutting remarks on modern capitalized Ireland.

Epilogue:
The Unromantic Seanchaí

Generally speaking, O'Flaherty's short stories mark a different literary world from that so often found in his novels. Séan Ó Faoláin once remarked how O'Flaherty's work "pulses with genuine hatred,"[26] are always full of violence, fury and passion. Indeed, there is a big difference between O'Flaherty's works in these two genres. Literary critic John Zneimer argues for a separate interpretation of O'Flaherty's short stories from his novels:

> The short stories turn to the country, to animals, and to nature. The society that appears is a part of nature. The characters are rough-hewn from Aran rock. The whole tone has changed... The novels can be described by a vocabulary of heat. The short stories can be described by light. Their surface is cold and shimmering. If the novels are marked by violence and melodrama and fury, O'Flaherty's short stories are best marked by their qualities of calmness, simplicity, and detachment. (146-7)

Simplicity and calmness are the keynote of O'Flaherty's short stories. The recurring violence is still there but the whole picture is represented with a different point of view. These well written vignettes are largely based on O'Flaherty's memories of his early experience in his native Aran Islands.

The overt sentimentality and use of melodrama employed in psychological realism, which are O'Flaherty's habitual techniques for expressing a "heightened level of intensity," are generally not the qualities found in his stories (O'Brien 1973, 95). To O'Flaherty's amazement, his literary reputation is largely based on his short stories though he started his literary career by writing novels in the 1920s.

Liam O'Flaherty's later life was silent and inactive, and there is also a change in style in his stories of the late period. Many of his more recent stories appear to be more artificial and less vivid than his earlier efforts, lacking the beauty of close observation and representation with powerful force and effect. Some of these later stories are even more overtly obvious in theme with artificial arrangement in plot and flat in effect than those written in the earlier period (Doyle 1971, 115). O'Flaherty's youthful energy seemed to wane in his later years; the unrest and fury in his frenzied emotions have been subdued to compassion and tranquility (Jeffares 234).

By and large Liam O'Flaherty's stories are representations of life embodied in living creatures, in the environment and in nature. His major concern is about how mankind and animals struggle to survive, revealing and exploring their basic primitive instinct and fundamental emotions, usually in passion. The everlasting cycle of life and the immortality of godly spirit in courage and endurance are prized highly in O'Flaherty's stories. His view of naturalism and realism unmasks his admiration for the profound elemental power in nature, said to mix with romanticism and realism in his own light.

Nevertheless, his treatment of the lives of peasants and animals in a cruel indifferent world often appears non-romantic, he rewards and celebrates the precious spirit, energy and motion in the process, which are immortal to him.   Consequently, the noble spirit is often found in rural areas where men and animals obtain less effect from the artificial civilization as in urban areas that render a sluggish world of inertia, full of hypocrisy, snobbishness and closed-mindedness (Gonzalez 89).

Ambivalence can be found in Liam O'Flaherty's life and works. His self-contradictory attitudes toward politics, such as Marxism, have been uncovered in his own autobiographies.   In one volume of his autobiographies, I Went to Russia, he recounts his disillusioned experience with socialism and Marxism that was adopted in Russia when he went there in the 1920s.   While many idealistic young Irishmen were joining James Connolly's Citizen Army or the Volunteers and preparing for the nationalist and socialist Easter Rising, O'Flaherty joined the Irish Guards of the British Army, serving in first World War until he was wounded and shell-shocked in France in 1917   He seems indifferent to the Easter Rising in 1916, O'Flaherty, however, became nostalgic about it later in his attack on Séan O'Casey's socialist critique of the same Rising in his play "The Plough and the Stars" as he considered that Séan did not do justice to James Connolly, Pádraig Pearse and their comrades (Cahalan 1991, 32).

Interestingly, the big difference in O'Flaherty's bilingual versions of some stories also uncover his ambiguous arrangement of major themes and treatment of characters.   O'Flaherty does not only revise some of the stories, but also rewrite some of them.   He does not intend to translate the stories into another language, but interpret them with a different viewpoint for some unknown reason(s). In many cases, O'Flaherty's Irish stories appear less artificial and bookish than their English counterparts, in that they use terse, direct and vibrant language (Murphy 1973, 20-5; de Bhaldraithe, 149-53).

O'Flaherty's attitudes toward women also reflect his ambivalence. In most cases, O'Flaherty regards women as "erotic and procreative objects for men" in sexist terms (Cahalan 1991, 41). In some of his stories on sexes, women are often portrayed as stereotyping roles and most of the time, women's inner qualities and mental development are ignored in stories. Similarly, in O'Flaherty's short narratives on early childhood, the characters are almost exclusively male. Even so, O'Flaherty still has some stories on powerful women over men such as "Red Barbara," and also takes a sympathetic approach of some stories about women being victims of men such as "The Outcast."

Seemingly, O'Flaherty did not maintain a consistency in his personal life and in his treatment of characters in stories. He once talked about his own self-contradictory senses in his personality by referring to an early experience of weaving a story about murdering a neighbouring woman in his childhood. And he claims that that experience has led to his divided self, the conflict of the good half and the dark half which he has to hide from people. Nevertheless, this mental conflict seems to transform itself into fruitful creative power and energy for O'Flaherty's writing.

Though Liam O'Flaherty's language in his short stories is sometimes viewed as plain, even dull, full of repetitions and clichés, his close connection with the Irish storytelling tradition is seen in some oral qualities of his stories. He tends to use a series of colourful imagery, being visual and aural in effect, and his choice of words is full of poetic rhythm.   Some passages display rich lyrical rhymes as found in poems; others show a vivid picture of the scene in stories as performed in films. It is perhaps not so surprising that O'Flaherty became very interested in films in later life.   Some of his works were adapted films and he also wrote screenplays for films.   In his autobiography, I Went to Russia, he enthused "I love the new art of the cinematograph" (224).[27]   To Liam O'Flaherty, then, it appears that films somehow best encapsulate the modern folktale, in that the speaking voice has transformed into visual images in the modern art (Kelly 1976, 39).

Liam O'Flaherty is a marvelous but long neglected, short story writer.   His genius has been best reflected in his short stories, and they are rightly considered to be the triumph of his art, highly praised by many critics.   In the variety of Liam O'Flaherty's short stories, life is represented and celebrated with the beauty of art.

Notes

[1] See Frank O'Connor, The Lonely Voice: A Study of the Short Story (Cleveland and New York: World Publishing Co., 1963) 37-39, qtd. in Doyle 1972: 50.

[2] We shall refer to some of the Gaelic motifs close to the surface of O'Flaherty's work in Chapter Two.

[3] See Liam O'Flaherty, Shame the Devil (London: Grayson and Grayson, 1934) 19, quoted. in Sheeran: 57.

[4] On the work of Synge, see Greene and Stephens.

[5] See Máirtín Ó Direáin's bilingual work Selected Poems (Tacar deanta) (Newbridge, Co. Kildare, Goldsmith, 1984).

[6] In this respect he is likely to resemble Rousseau's belief in the basic instincts of human beings but he does not follow Rousseau's Christian God but a "new God-knowledge" of his own like D. H. Lawrence. For the discussion of Rousseau and Lawrence, please see Robert P. H. Hsu, Duality in D. H. Lawrence's Art (Taipei: The Graduate Institute of Western Literature and Languages, Tamkang University, 1979).

[7] See William Troy, "The Position of Liam O'Flaherty," Bookman Mar. 1929: 7, qtd. in O'Brien 1973: 94.

[8] The translation of Irish into English is quoted in Murphy's

discussion on the two versions of Liam O'Flaherty's English and Irish stories.   See Maureen O'Rourke Murphy, "The Double Visions of Liam O'Flaherty," Éire-Ireland 8.3 (1973): 20-5.

[9] See Frank O'Connor, "A Good Short Story Must Be News," New York Times Book Review 10 June 1956: 20, qtd. in Mercier 1964: 105.

[10] Kennelly once used this passage as his example for showing O'Flaherty's poetic qualities in his book article "Liam O'Flaherty: The Unchained Storm.   A View of His Short Stories," The Irish Short Story, ed. Patrick Rafroidi and Terence Brown (Gerrards Cross: Colin Smythe, 1979) 175-187.

[11] See Cahalan 1991, 55-6.   In his studies on Liam O'Flaherty's short fiction, James M. Calahan connects O'Flaherty's major themes and motifs with Darwin's theory of evolution and Marxism.

[12] This phrase also serves as the title for one O'Flaherty's autobiographies: Shame the Devil (London: Grayson and Grayson, 1934), qtd. in Thompson: 84.

[13] See Seán Ó Faoláin, "Don Quixote O'Flaherty," The Bell Jun. 1941: 28-36.

[14] In Chinese philosophy, Yin and Yang are two elemental forces in the Universe, both of which must be kept a balance and the Universe is an everlasting cycle of birth and death.   The natural law is not based on the belief of divine revelation of Christian God but a more mysterious Creator.

[15] See Liam O'Flaherty, Shame the Devil (London: Grayson and Grayson, 1934) 10, 55, qtd. in Cahalan 1991: 55.

[16] On a reduced scale, we can see this echoed in the Gaelic proverb "Nature breaks through the eyes of the cat" (Briseann an díchas tré shúile an chait).

[17] See The Irish Statesman 18th Oct. 1924: 171, qtd. in Kennelly: 177.

[18] One can detect an echo of the Gaelic aspect of life on Aran in the form of Oisín, son of Fionn mac Cumhaill, following his return from the Land of Youth.

[19] Once more, one feels a sense of Gaelic folk philosophy here, reminiscent of Blasket Island writer Muiris Ó Súileabháin's "Twenty years a growing, Twenty years in flower, Twenty years decaying, Twenty years without prosperity."

[20] See Vivian Mercier, introduction, The Stories of Liam O'Flaherty, by Liam O'Flaherty (New York: Devin-Adair, 1956) viii, qtd. in Doyle 1971: 47.

[21] For further information about the White Snake myth, see Anne M. Birrell, Chinese Mythology: An Introduction (Baltimore: John Hopkins University Press, 1993).

[22] See Frank O'Connor, "A Good Short Story Must Be News," The New York Times Book Review 10 June 1956: 1, 20, qtd. in Doyle 1971: 58.

[23] See Liam O'Flaherty, A Tourist's Guide to Ireland (London: Mandrake Press, 1929) 19, qtd. in Cahalan 1991: 37.

[24] See Liam O'Flaherty, Two Years (New York: Harcourt and Brace, 1930) 61, qtd. in Cahalan 1991: 37.

[25] The same is also true of Exile, the early twentieth-century Gaelic novel by Pádraig Ó Conaire based, to a large degree in seedy

London.

26   See Seán Ó Faoláin, "Don Quixote O'Flaherty," <u>The Bell</u> Jun. 1941:
      28-36, qtd. in Zneimer: 146.

27   This sentence is quoted in Cahalan 1991: 57.

Works Cited

I. Primary Sources

Collection of Short Stories

(The abbreviation for the story collection used in this book is given in parenthesis; the edition is in many cases not the first edition)

The Tent (TT). London: Cape, 1926.

Spring Sowing (SP). London: Cape, 1927.

The Mountain Tavern (MT). New York: Harcourt and Brace, 1929.

The Wild Swan and Other Stories (WS). London: Joiner & Steele, 1932.

Two Lovely Beasts (TL). London: Gollancz, 1948.

The Stories of Liam O'Flaherty (SL). New York: Devin-Adair, 1956.

Dúil (DL). Baile Átha Cliath: Sáirséal agus Dill, 1962.

Selected Short Stories of Liam O'Flaherty (SS). London: New English Library, 1970.

More Short Stories of Liam O'Flaherty (MS). London: New English Library, 1971.

The Pedlar's Revenge (PR). Dublin: Wolfhound Press, 1996.

Autobiography

Two Years.   London: Cape, 1930.

I Went to Russia.   London: Cape, 1931.

Shame the Devil.   London: Grayson and Grayson, 1934.

Letters

The Letters of Liam O'Flaherty.   Ed.   Angeline A. Kelly.   Dublin: Wolfhound Press, 1996.

Booklets

A Tourist's Guide to Ireland.   London: Mandrake Press, 1929.

II. Secondary Sources

Bates, H. E.   Edward Garnett.   London: Parrish, 1950.

Cahalan, James M.   The Irish Novel: A Critical History.   Dublin: Gill & Macmillan, 1988.

---.   Liam O'Flaherty: A Study of the Short Fiction.   Boston: Twayne, 1991.

Costello, Peter.   Liam O'Flaherty's Ireland.   Dublin: Wolfhound Press, 1996.

Davis, Rhys.   Introduction.   The Wild Swan and Other Stories.   By Liam O'Flaherty.   London: Joiner & Steele, 1932.

De Bhaldraithe, Thomas.   "Liam O'Flaherty—Translator(?)."   Éire-Ireland
    (Summer 1968): 149-53.

Doyle, Paul A.   Liam O'Flaherty.   New York: Twayne, 1971.

---.   Liam O'Flaherty: An Annotated Bibliography.   New York: Whitston
    Publishing Co., 1972.

Gonzalez, Alexander.   "Liam O'Flaherty's Urban Short Stories."   Etudes
    Irlandaises 12.1 (June 1987): 85-91.

Greene, David and Edward M. Stephens.   J. M. Synge 1871-1909.   New
    York: Macmillan, 1959.

Jeffares, A. Norman.   Anglo-Irish Literature.   London: Macmillan, 1982.

Jefferson, George.   Liam O'Flaherty: A Descriptive Bibliography of His
    Works.   Dublin: Wolfhound Press, 1993.

Hampton, Angeline A.   "Liam O'Flaherty's Short Stories — Visual and
    Aural Effects."   English Studies 55 (1974): 110-17.

Hildebidle, John.   Five Irish Writers: The Errand of Keeping Alive.
    Cambridge: Harvard UP, 1989.

Hogan, Robert, ed.   Dictionary of Irish Literature.   Westport, Connecticut:
    Greenwood Press, 1979.

Kelly, Angeline A.   Introduction.   The Pedlar's Revenge.   By Liam
    O'Flaherty.   Dublin: Wolfhound Press, 1996.

---.   Liam O'Flaherty the Storyteller.   London: Macmillan, 1976.

Kennelly, Brendan.   "Liam O'Flaherty: The Unchained Storm: A View of
    His Short Stories."   The Irish Short Story.   Ed. Patrick Rafroidi and
    Terence Brown.   Gerrards Cross: Colin Smythe, 1979.   175-87.

Lane, Denis and Carol McCrory Lane, ed.   Modern Irish Literature: A Library
    of Literary Criticism.   New York: Ungar Publishing Company, 1988.

McRedmond, Louis, ed.   Modern Irish Lives: Dictionary of 20th-Century Biography.   Dublin: Gill and Macmillan, 1996.

Mercier, Vivian.   Introduction.   The Stories of Liam O'Flaherty.   New York: Devin-Adair, 1956.

---.   "The Irish Short Story and Oral Tradition."   The Celtic Cross: Studies in Irish Culture and Literature.   Eds.   Ray B. Browne, William John Rossell and John Loftus.   West Lafayette: Purdue University Press, 1964.   98-116.

Murphy, Maureen.   "The Double Vision of Liam O'Flaherty." Éire-Ireland 8.3 (1973): 20-25.

---.   "'The Salted Goat': Devil's Bargain or Fable of Faithfulness." Rev. of The Pedlar's Revenge.   Ed. A. A. Kelly.   Canadian Journal of Irish Studies 5.2 (1979): 60-61.

Murray, Michael H.   "Liam O'Flaherty and the Speaking Voice." Studies in Short Fiction 5 (1968): 154-162.

O'Brien, H. J.   "Liam O'Flaherty's Ego-Anarchist."   University of Dayton Review 7.2 (1971): 73-75.

---.   Liam O'Flaherty.   Lewisburg: Bucknell University Press, 1973.

O'Connor, Frank.   "A Good Short Story Must Be News."   The New York Times Book Review 10 June 1956:1, 20.

---.   The Lonely Voice: A Study of the Short Story.   New York: The World Publishing Company, 1962.

O'Connor, Helene.   "Liam O'Flaherty: Literary Ecologist."   Éire-Ireland 7.2 (1972): 47-54.

Ó Direáin, Máirtín.   Selected Poems (Tacar Déanta).   Trans.   Tomás Mac Siomóin and Douglas Sealy.   Newbridge, Co. Kildare: Goldsmith, 1984.

Ó Faoláin, Seán. "Don Quixote O'Flaherty," The Bell Jun. 1941: 28-36.

Saul, George Brandon. "Wild Sowing: The Short Stories of Liam O'Flaherty." A Review of English Literature 4.3 (1963): 108-113.

Scher, Amy. "Preaching an Ecological Conscience: Liam O'Flaherty's Short Stories." Éire-Ireland 29.2 (Summer 1994): 113-22.

Sheeran, Patrick F. The Novels of Liam O'Flaherty: A Study in Romantic Realism. Dublin: Wolfhound, 1976.

Thompson, Richard J. "The Sage Who Deep in Central Nature Delves: Liam O'Flaherty's Short Stories." Éire- Ireland 18.1 (Spring 1983): 80-97.

Troy, William. "The Position of Liam O'Flaherty." Bookman Mar. 1929: 7-11.

Washburn, Judith. "Objective Narration in Liam O'Flaherty's Short Stories." Éire-Ireland 24.3 (Fall 1989): 120-125.

Welch, Robert. The Oxford Companion to Irish Literature. Oxford: Claredon Press, 1996.

Wright, Charles. "'Red Barbara and Liam O'Flaherty: Weaver of Words, Weaver of Worlds." The Canadian Journal of Irish Studies 21.2 (December 1995): 32-37.

Wyllie John Cook. "Mankind in Animals." Saturday Review June 30 1956: 11.

Zneimer, John. The Literary Vision of Liam O'Flaherty. New York: Syracuse UP, 1970.

Appendix:
Liam O'Flaherty: A Select Bibliography

I. General Sources

(1) Books

Baumgarten, Rolf. Bibliography of Irish Linguistics and Literature. Dublin: Dublin Institute for Advanced Studies, 1986.

Doyle, Paul A. Liam O'Flaherty: An Annotated Bibliography. New York: Troy, 1972.

Eager, Alan R. A Guide to Irish Bibliographical Material. London: Library Association, 1980.

Finneran, Richard et al. Recent Research on Anglo-Irish Writers: A Supplement to Anglo-Irish Literature : A Review of Research. Modern Language Association of America, 1970.

Harmon, Maurice. Select Bibliography for the Study of Anglo-Irish Literature and Its Backgrounds. Dublin: Wolfhound, 1977.

Hayes, H. J. Manuscript Sources for the History of Irish Civilization. Boston: G. K. Hall, 1965.

Jefferson, George. Liam O'Flaherty: A Descriptive Bibliography of His Works. Dublin: Wolfhound, 1993.

Kersnowski, Frank L., C. W. Spinks, and Laird Loomis, eds.   A Bibliography of Modern Irish and Anglo-Irish Literature.   Dublin: Trinity University Press, 1976.

O'Malley, William T.   Anglo-Irish Literature: A Bibliography of Dissertation 1873-1989.   Westport: Greenwood, 1990.

(2) Journals

(a) English

Canadian Journal of Irish Studies (CJIS).   Vancouver: Canadian Association of Irish Studies.

Éire-Ireland, a Journal of Irish Studies (Éire).   St. Paul: Irish American Cultural Institute.

Etudes Irlandaises (Etudes).   Gaeliana Cahiers--Centre d'Etudes Anglo-Irlandaises: Université de Haute Bretagne.

Irish University Review (IUR).   Shannon, Ireland: Irish University Press.

(b) Irish

An Nua Fhilíocht.   Maigh Nuad: An Sagart.

An tUltach.   Beal Feirste: An tUltach.

Comhar.   Baile Átha Cliath: Comhar Teoranta.

Feasta.   Baile Átha Cliath: Conradh na Gaeilge.

Irisleabhar Mhá Nuad.   Baile Átha Cliath: An Clochomhar.

II. Primary Sources

(1) Works in English

(a) Novels

Thy Neighbour's Wife. London: Cape, 1923; New York: Boni and Liveright, 1924.

The Black Soul. London: Cape, 1924, 1936; New York: Boni and Liveright, 1925; Travellers' Library Edition, 1928, 1931; Bath: Lythway Press, 1972.

The Informer. London: Cape, 1925, 1929, 1949; John Lane, 1935; Landsborough Publications, 1958, 1964; The Folio Society, 1961; New York: Knopf, 1925; New American Library, 1961, 1970, 1971.

Mr. Gilhooley. London: Cape, 1926; New York: Harcourt and Brace, 1927; Dublin: Wolfhound, 1991.

The Wilderness. London: serialised in The Humanist Jan. 1927, 17-25; Feb. 1927, 69-78; Mar. 1927, 121-9; Apr. 1927, 175-82; May 1927, 225-34; June 1927, 275-85.

The Assassin. London: Cape, 1928, Landsborough Publications, 1959; New York: Harcourt and Brace, 1928.

The House of Gold. London: Cape, 1929; New York: Harcourt and Brace, 1930.

The Return of the Brute. London: Mandrake Press, 1929; New York: Harcourt and Brace, 1930.

The Puritan. London: Cape, 1931; New York: Harcourt and Brace, 1930.

Skerrett. London: Gollancz, 1932; New York: Long and Smith, 1932.

The Martyr.   London: Gollancz, 1935; New York: Macmillan, 1933.

Hollywood Cemetery.   London: Gollancz, 1935.

Famine.   London: Gollancz, 1937; Landsborough Publications, 1959, 1966; New York: Random House, 1937.

Land.   London: Gollancz, 1946; New York: Random House, 1946.

Insurrection.   London: Gollancz, 1950; Landsborough Publications, 1959; Boston: Little, Brown, 1951.

(b) Collections of Short Stories

Spring Sowing.   London: Cape, 1924; Travellers' Library Edition, 1927, 1929, 1931, 1935; New York: Knopf, 1926.

The Tent.   London: Cape, 1926.

The Mountain Tavern.   London: Cape, 1929; New York: Harcourt and Brace, 1929.

The Short Stories of Liam O'Flaherty.   London: Cape, 1937, 1948; Four Square Books, The New English Library, 1966, 1970, 1986.

Two Lovely Beasts.   London: Gollancz, 1948; Consul Books, 1961; New York: Devin-Adair, 1950.

The Stories of Liam O'Flaherty.   New York: Devin-Adair, 1956.

The Wounded Cormorant and Other Stories.   New York: Norton, 1956, 1973.

Liam O'Flaherty: Selected Stories.   Ed. Devin A. Garrity.   New York: Signet Book, The New American Library, 1958.

The Short Stories of Liam O'Flaherty.   London: Brown, Watson, 1961.

B. M. Naughton / Liam O'Flaherty Short Stories.   London: Pergamon Press, New English Library, 1968.

Selected Short Stories of Liam O'Flaherty.   London: New English Library, 1970.

Irish Portraits: 14 Short Stories by Liam O'Flaherty.   London: Sphere Books, 1970.

More Short Stories of Liam O'Flaherty.   London: New English Library, 1971.

The Pedlar's Revenge.   Dublin: Wolfhound, 1976, 1982, 1989, 1993, 1996.

(c) Autobiography

Full-length Works

Two Years.   London: Cape, 1930; New York: Harcourt and Brace, 1930.

I Went to Russia.   London: Cape, 1931; New York: Harcourt and Brace, 1931.

Shame the Devil.   London: Grayson and Grayson, 1934.

Autobiographical Articles

"My Experience (1896-1923)."   Now and Then Dec. 1923: 14-15.

"My Life of Adventure."   T.P.'s Weekly 20 Oct. 1928: 756.

"Autobiographical Note."   Ten Contemporaries.   Ed. John Gawsworth. London, 1933.   139-43.

"I Go to Sea."   Esquire Sep. 1952: 38-9.

(d) Biography

The Life of Tim Healy.   London: Cape, 1927; New York: Harcourt and Brace, 1927.

(e) Booklets

A Tourist's Guide to Ireland.   London: Mandrake Press, 1929, 1930.

Joseph Conrad: An Appreciation.   New York, 1929; London: Blue Moon
    Booklets, 1930.

A Cure for Unemployment.   London: Blue Moon Booklets, No. 8, E. Lahr,
    1931; New York: Julian Press, 1931.

The Ecstasy of Angus.   London: Joiner and Steele, 1931.

(f) Poetry

"The Blow."   Bell 19 May 1954: 9-22.

"Desire."   Bell 19 Jul. 1954: 48-50.

"The Sniper."   Scholastic Oct. 18, 1956: 18.

(g) Drama

Darkness: A Tragedy in Three Acts.   London: Archer, 1926.

(h) Introductions

Introduction.   Bitter Water.   By Heinrich Hauser.   Trans. Patrick Kirwan.
    London: Wishart and Company, 1930.

Introduction.   Six Cartoons.   By Alfred Lowe.   London: W. and G.
    Foyle, 1930. 7-8.

Foreword.   The Stars, The World, and The Women.   By Rhys Davies.
    London: William Jackson, 1930.   7-9.

(i) Essays, Letters and Book Reviews

"Jim Larkin the Rebel."   The Plain People 18 June 1922: 4.

"The Blurb Again."   Now and Then Dec. 1923: 11.

"Sinclair Lewis's Free Air."   The Irish Statesman 5 Apr. 1924: 116.

"Adrien Le Corbeau's The Forest Giant."   The Irish Statesman 5 Apr. 1924: 116.

"Vera Britain's Not without Honour."   The Irish Statesman 5 Apr. 1924: 118.

"H. G. Wells' A Life."   The Irish Statesman 7 June 1924: 402, 404.

"National Energy."   The Irish Statesman 18 Oct. 1924: 171.

"Trimblerigg, by Laurence Houseman."   Now and Then Christmas 1924: 29-30.

"Mr. Tasker's Gods."   The Irish Statesman 7 Mar. 1925: 827-8.

"A View of Irish Culture."   The Irish Statesman 20 June 1925: 460-1.

"Peadar O'Donnell's Storms and H. N. Brailsford's Socialism for Today."   The   Irish Statesman 9 Jan. 1926: 556, 568.

"The Plough and the Stars."   The Irish Statesman 20 Feb. 1926: 739-40.

"Fascism or Communism."   The Irish Statesman: 8 May 1926: 231-2.

"Review of Ethel Manning's Sounding Brass."   The Irish Statesman 5 June 1926: 360, 362.

"Literary Criticism in Ireland."   The Irish Statesman 4 Sep. 1926: 711.

"Art Criticism."   The Irish Statesman 1 Oct. 1927: 348.

"The Waratahs."   The Irish Statesman 19 Nov. 1927: 253-4.

"Writing in Gaelic."   The Irish Statesman 17 Dec. 1927: 348.

"Red Ship."   New Republic 23 Sep. 1931: 147-50.

"Kingdom of Kerry."   Fortnightly Review Aug. 1932: 212-18.

"The Irish Censorship."   The American Spectator Yearbook.   Eds. G. Jean Nathan and Theodore Dreiser.   New York, 1934.   131-4.

"Irish Housekeeping."   New Statesman and Nation Feb. 1936: 186.

"Good Soldiers Play Safe."   Esquire May 1942: 23, 120-2.

"Village Ne'er-do-well."   Esuqire Sep. 1945: 53-4.

"Personalities by Nimrod."   Irish Tatler and Sketch Apr. 1949: 36, 75.

Letters to Edward Garnett, May 5, 1923 to March 3, 1932.   In the Manuscript Collection of The Academic Center Library, The University of Texas, Austin.

The Letters of Liam O'Flaherty.   Ed.   A. A. Kelly.   Dublin: Wolfhound, 1993, 1996.

(2) Works in Irish

(a) Collection of Short Stories

Dúil.   Baile Átha Cliath: Sáirseal and Dill 1953, 1962, 1966.

(b) Short Stories in Periodicals

"Fód."   The Dublin Magazine 11 Nov. 1924: 882-3.

"Bás na Bó."   Fáinne an Lae 18 Iúl. 1925: 5.

"An tAonach."   Fáinne an Lae 5 M.Fómh 1925.

"Daoine Bochta."   Fáinne an Lae 29 Lún. 1925: 3.

"Throideadar go Fíochmar."   The Irish Press 6 Meith. 1946.

"An Chulaith Nua."   The Irish Press 21 Meith. 1946: 2.

"Teangabháil."   Comhar Iúl. 1946.

(c) Poetry

"Smaointe I gCéin."   The Dublin Magazine 11 Nol. 1924: 330.

"Na Blátha Craige."   Nuabhéarsaíocht 1938-48.   Ed. Séan Ó Tuama. Dublin, 35.

(d) Essays and Letters

"Briseann an Dúchas."   The Irish Press 30 May 1946: 2.

"Throideamar Go Fíochmhar."   The Irish Press 6 June 1946: 2.

"An Braon Broghach."   Comhar Bealtaine 1949: 5, 30.

"Ag Casadh le Padraig Ó Conaire."   Comhar Aibrean 1953: 3-6.

(e) Translation from Irish

Padraig Ó Conaire, "The Agony of the World."   The Adelphi Sep. 1925: 250-60.

III. Secondary Sources

(1) Film

Nichols, Dudley, adapt.   The Informer.   By Liam O'Flaherty.   Theatre Arts, 1935.

Musso, Jesse, dir.   Le Puritain.   Perf.   Jean-Louis Barrantt, Pierre Fresnay, and Vivian Romance.   Derby Production, 1937.

Ford, John, dir.   The Informer.   By Liam O'Flaherty.   Perf.   Victor McLaglen, Preston Foster, Heather Angel, and Margot Grahame. Videocassette. Vidamerica, Inc., 1987.

(2) Some Criticism in English

(a) Articles

Bhaldraithe, Thomas de. "Liam O'Flaherty — Translator(?)." Éire-Ireland (Summer 1968): 149-53.

Broderick, John. "Liam O'Flaherty: A Partial View." Hibernia 19 Dec. 1969: 17.

Crawford, John. "Liam O'Flaherty's Black and White World." The Irish Press 1 Aug. 1953: 4.

Daniels, William. "Introduction to the Present State of Criticism of Liam O'Flaherty's Collection of Short Stories: Dúil." Éire-Ireland 23.2 (Summer 1988): 122-134.

---. "The Diction of Desire: Liam O'Flaherty's Dúil.'" Éire-Ireland 24.4 (Winter 1989): 75-88.

Davis, Rhys. Introduction. The Wild Swan and Other Stories. By Liam O'Flaherty. London: Joiner & Steele, 1932.

Deane, Paul. "The Ambiguous Rebel: Liam O'Flaherty's The Martyr." Notes on Modern Irish Literature 7.2 (Fall 1995): 22-28.

Donnelly, Brian. "A Nation Gone Wrong: Liam O'Flaherty's Vision of Modern Ireland." Studies: An Irish Quarterly Review 63 (1974): 71-81.

Doyle, Paul A. "O'Flaherty's Real View of The Informer." The Dublin Magazine 8.3: 67-70.

---. "A Liam O'Flaherty Checklist." Twentieth Century Literature 13 (April 1967): 49-51.

Eglington, John. "Irish Letter." The Dial May 1927: 407-410.

Freyer, Grattan. "The Irish Contribution." The Modern Age. Ed. Boris
  Ford. Baltimore: Penguin, 1961. 197, 205-207.

---. "Change Naturally: The Fiction of O'Flaherty, Ó Faoláin, McGahern."
  Éire-Ireland 18.1 (Spring 1983): 138-144.

Friberg, Hedda. "Women in Three Works by Liam O'Flaherty: In Search
  of an Egalitarian Impulse." Homage to Ireland: Aspects of Culture,
  Literature and Language. Ed. Birgit Bramsback. Uppsala: Univ.
  Uppsala, 1990. 45-61.

Gonzalez, Alexander. "Liam O'Flaherty's Urban Short Stories." Etudes
  Irlandaises 12.1 (June 1987): 85-91.

Greene, David H. "New Heights." Commonweal 29 June 1956: 328.

Hackett, Francis. "Liam O'Flaherty as Novelist." On Judging Books.
  New York, 1947. 288-93.

Hampton, Angeline A. "Liam O'Flaherty: Additions to the Checklist."
  Éire-Ireland 6.4 (1971): 87-94.

---. "Liam O'Flaherty's Short Stories--Visual and Aural Effects."
  English Studies 55 (1974): 440-47.

Harte, Liam. "Free State Interrogators: Liam O'Flaherty and Frank
  O'Connor, The Informer by Liam O'Flaherty and My Father's Son by
  Frank O'Connor." Irish Studies Review 8.2 (2000): 233-38.

Hatcher, Harlan. "Motion Picture Drama: Liam O'Flaherty." Modern
  Dramas. New York: Harcourt and Brace, 1944. 195-98.

Heaney, Dermot. "The O'Flaherty Novel: A Problem of Critical
  Approach." Etudes Irlandaises 20.2 (1995): 45-55.

Higgins, Md. "Liam O'Flaherty and Peadar O'Donnell—Images of Rural
  Community." Crane Bag 1985: 41-48.

Hoult, Norah. "Liam O'Flaherty and the Irish Scene." Bookman June 1934: 170.

Hughes, Riley. "Two Irish Writers." America 2 Sep. 1950: 560-1.

Hynes, Frank J. "The Troubles in Ireland." Saturday Review of Literature 25 May 1946: 12.

Kelleher, John V. "Irish Literature Today." Atlantic Monthly Mar. 1945: 70-6; The Bell 1945: 337-53.

Kelly, Angeline A. Introduction. The Pedlar's Revenge. By Liam O'Flaherty. Dublin: Wolfhound, 1976, 1996.

---. "O'Flaherty on the Shelf." Hibernia 20 Nov 1970: 8.

Kennelly, Brendan. "Liam O'Flaherty: The Unchained Storm: A View of His Short Stories." The Irish Short Story. Ed. Patrick Rafroidi and Terence Brown. Gerrards Cross: Colin Smythe, 1979. 175-87.

Kiely, Benedict. "Liam O'Flaherty: A Story of Discontent." Month Sep. 1949: 184-193.

---. Rev. of The Literary Vision of Liam O'Flaherty. By John Zneimer. The New York Times 3 Jan. 1971: 4.

Kilroy, James F. "Setting the Standards: Writers of the 1920s and 1930s." The Irish Short Story: A Critical History. Ed. James F. Kilroy. Boston: Twayne, 1984. 95-114.

Klaus, H. Gustav. "'Carry the Wild Rose of Insurrection': Liam O'Flaherty's Novels on the Easter Rising." Etudes Irlandaises 14.1 (June 1989): 117-126.

Lynch, Rachael Sealy. "'Soft Talk' and 'An Alien Grip': Gallagher's Rhetoric of Control in O'Flaherty's The Informer." Journal of Irish Literature 23.2 (Fall-Winter 1993): 260-68.

MacDonagh, Donagh. Afterword. The Informer. By Liam O'Flaherty. New York: New American Library, 1961.

Marchbanks, Paul. "Lessons in Lunacy: Mental Illness in Liam O'Flaherty's Famine." New Hibernia Review. 10.2 (2006): 92-105.

Mellamphy, Ninian. Rev. of Liam O'Flaherty the Storyteller. By A. A. Kelly. The Canadian Journal of Irish Studies 4.1 (1978): 74-77.

Mercier, Vivian. Introduction. The Stories of Liam O'Flaherty. New York: Devin-Adair, 1956.

---. "The Irish Short Story and Oral Tradition." The Celtic Cross: Studies in Irish Culture and Literature. Eds. Ray B. Browne, William John Rosselli, and John Loftus. West Lafayette: Purdue University Press, 1964. 98-116.

---. "Man Against Nature: The Novels of Liam O'Flaherty." Wascana Review 1996: 37-46.

Moseley, Maboth. "The Humanity of Liam O'Flaherty." The Humanist May 1927: 223.

Murphy, Maureen. "The Double Vision of Liam O'Flaherty." Éire-Ireland 8.3 (1973): 20-25.

---. "'The Salted Goat': Devil's Bargain or Fable of Faithfulness." Rev. of The Pedlar's Revenge. Ed. A. A. Kelly. Canadian Journal of Irish Studies 5.2 (1979): 60-61.

Murray, Michael H. "Liam O'Flaherty and the Speaking Voice." Studies in Short Fiction 5 (1968): 154-162.

O'Brien, H. J. "Liam O'Flaherty's Ego-Anarchist." University of Dayton Review 7.2 (1971): 73-75.

---. "Liam O'Flaherty's The Informer." The Dublin Magazine 1972: 56-58.

O'Connor, Frank.   "A Good Short Story Must Be News."   The New York Times Book Review 10 June 1956: 1,20.

O'Connor, Helene.   "Liam O'Flaherty: Literary Ecologist."   Éire-Ireland 7.2 (1972): 47-54.

Ó Faoláin, Seán.   "Don Quixote O'Flaherty."   The Bell June 1941: 28-36.

---.   "Fifty Years of Irish Writing."   Studies Spring 1962: 102-3.

---.   "Speaking of Books: Dyed Irish."   The New York Times 12 May 1968.

---.   "Dúil: Liam O Flaithearta."   The Pleasures of Gaelic Literature.   Ed. John   Jordan.   Cork: Mercier, 1977.   111-19.

O'Glaisne, Risteard.   "Rogha Teanga: Ó Flaithearta Agus an Gaeilge."   Comhar 39.6 (1980): 16-17.

O'Hara, Patricia.   "James M. Cahalan: Liam O'Flaherty: A Study of the Short Fiction."   Rev. of Liam O'Flaherty: A Study of the Short Fiction.   By James M. Cahalan.   Studies in Short Fiction 29.2 (Spring 1992): 228.

Ó hEithir, Breandan.   "Liam Ó Flatharta agus a Dhuchas."   Willie the Plain Pint Agus an Papa.   Cork: Mercier, 1977.   65-76.

Phillips, T.   "A Study in Grotesques: Transformations of the Human in the Writing of Liam O'Flaherty."   Gothic Studies. 7.1 (2005): 41-52.

Ryan, Richard.   "Liam O'Flaherty: A Blackened Soul."   Hibernia 10 May 1974: 24.

Saul, George Brandon.   "Wild Sowing: The Short Stories of Liam O'Flaherty."   A Review of English Literature 4.3 (1963): 108-113.

Scher, Amy.   "Preaching and Ecological Conscience: Liam O'Flaherty's Short Stories."   Éire-Ireland 29.2 (Summer 1994): 113-22.

Swinnerton, Frank. "Liam O'Flaherty's New Novel." Now and Then Winter 1929: 28-29.

Thompson, Richard J. "The Sage Who Deep in Central Nature Delves: Liam O'Flaherty's Short Stories." Éire-Ireland 18.1 (Spring 1983): 80-97.

Troy, William. "The Position of Liam O'Flaherty." Bookman Mar. 1929: 7-11.

---. "Two Years." Bookman Nov. 1930: 322-3.

---. "Mr. O'Flaherty's Development." Nation Aug. 1933: 165.

Warren, Clarence Henry. Rev. of The Mountain Tavern. By Liam O'Flaherty. Bookman Sep. 1929: 313.

---. "Liam O'Flaherty." Bookman Jan. 1930: 235-6.

Washburn, Judith. "Objective Narration in Liam O'Flaherty's Short Stories." Éire-Ireland 24.3 (Fall 1989): 120-125.

Wright, Charles. "'Red Barbara' and Liam O'Flaherty: Weaver of Words, Weaver of Worlds." The Canadian Journal of Irish Studies 21.2 (December 1995): 32-37.

Wyllie John Cook. "Mankind in Animals." Saturday Review June 30 1956: 11.

Zneimer, John N. "Liam O'Flaherty: The Pattern of Spiritual Crisis in His Art." Dissertation Abstract 28 (1967): 701A-702A.

(b) Books

Cahalan, James M. Liam O'Flaherty: A Study of the Short Fiction. Boston: Twayne, 1991.

Doyle, Paul A. Liam O'Flaherty. New York: Twayne, 1971.

Friberg, Hedda. An Old Order and a New: the Spilt World of Liam O'Flaherty's Novels. Uppsala: Uppsala University, 1996.

Hildebidle, John. Five Irish Writers: The Errand of Keeping Alive. Cambridge: Harvard UP, 1989.

Kelly, A. A. Liam O'Flaherty the Storyteller. London: Macmillan, 1976.

O'Brien, James Howard. Liam O'Flaherty. Lewisburg: Bucknell University Press, 1973.

Sheeran, Patrick F. The Novels of Liam O'Flaherty: A Study in Romantic Realism. Dublin: Wolfhound, 1976.

Val Baker, Denys, ed. Writers of To-day. London: Sidgwick, 1948.

Votteler, Thomas and Shannon J. Young. Short Story Criticism: Excerpts from Criticism of the Works of Short Fiction Writers. Detroit: Gale Research Inc., 1990.

Zneimer, John. The Literary Vision of Liam O'Flaherty. New York: Syracuse UP, 1970.

(c) Dissertation on Liam O'Flaherty's Work

Averill, Deborah Moore. The Theme of Escape in the Short Stories of Liam O'Flaherty, Frank O'Connor and Seán_Ó Faoláin. Diss. Rochester, 1976. Ann Arbor: UMI, 1976. 7623975.

Banks, Sheryl Gail. "Limeys in the Orange Grove: the British Novel in Los Angeles." Diss. University of Southern California, 1987.

Browne, Joseph Peter. Aspect of the Art of Liam O'Flaherty. Diss. Pennsylvania, 1978. Ann Arbor: UMI, 1979. 7908713.

Canedo, Anthony. Liam O'Flaherty: Introduction and Analysis. Diss. Washington, 1965. Ann Arbor: UMI, 1966. 6605818.

Davenport, Gary Tolleson. Four Irish Writers in Time of Civil War: Liam O'Flaherty, Frank O'Connor, Seán_Ó Faoláin, and Elizabeth Bowen. Diss. South Carolina, 1971. Ann Arbor: UMI, 1972. 7212003.

Detroy, Virginia M. Wickenkamp. An Evaluation and Thematic Assessment of the Short Fiction of Liam O'Flaherty. Diss. University of Louisville, 1971. Ann Arbor: UMI, 1971. 1302588.

Dockrell-Grunberg, Susanne. "Studien Zur Struktur Moderner Anglo-Irischer Kurzgeschichten." Diss. Tubingen, 1967.

Donnelly, Brian. "Liam O'Flaherty: A Critical Study of His Art." M.A. Diss. Department of Art History and Theory. University of Essex, 1973.

Friberg, Hedda Ingrid. An Old Order and a New: The Split World of Liam O'Flaherty's Novels. Diss. Uppsala: Uppsala University, 1996.

Gonzalez, Alexander George. The Motif of Physical Paralysis in the Literature of the Irish Renaissance: Studies in Martyn, Moore, Corkery, and O'Flaherty. Diss. Oregon, 1982. Ann Arbor: UMI, 1982. 8224842.

Hampton, Angeline A. "The Short Stories of Liam O'Flaherty." Diss. Geneve, 1971.

Hinners, Richard Graham. An Analysis of the Effects of Varying Focus in Solo Oral Interpretation. Diss. Wayne State University, 1981. Ann Arbor: UMI, 1982. 8209312.

Jackson, Robin Heavner. "Troubled Trinity Love, Religion, and Patriotism in Liam O'Flaherty's First Novel, Thy Neighbour's Wife." Diss. East Tennessee State University, 2002.

Liebrich, Diana Salome. "Liam O'Flaherty: "Famine": Mediinhistorische Betrachtung der Irishen Hungersnot." Diss. Köln Universität, 2007.

McNamara, Donald.   "Flann O'Brien and Liam O'Flaherty: Refashioning Myth and Nationhood."   Diss. Catholic University of America, 2001.

O'Brien, H. J.   "The Representation of Religion in the Fiction of Liam O'Flaherty and Francis Stuart."   Diss.   Trinity-Dublin, 1966.

O'Connor, Helene Louise.   Liam O'Flaherty: Literary Ethologist.   Diss. New York University, 1970.   Ann Arbor: UMI, 1971.   7105618.

Saagpakk, Paul Frudrich.   "Psychopathological Elements in British Novels From 1890 to 1930."   Diss.   Columbia, 1966.

Tschann, Sylvie Marie.   "Man's Divine Destiny in Liam O'Flaherty's Short Stories."   Diss.   Nashville: Vanderbilt University, 1971.

Wahlert, Ernst Henry, Jr.   "Liam O'Flaherty: Social Critic of Ireland." Diss. Dallas: Southern Methodist University, 1948.

Zneimer, John Nicolas.   Liam O'Flaherty: the Pattern of Spiritual Crisis in His Art.   Diss.   Wisconsin, 1966.   Ann Arbor: UMI, 1967. 6605960.

(3) Some Criticism in Irish

(a) Articles

Bhaldraithe, Tomas de.   "Ó Flaithearta--Aistritheoir."   Comhar Bealtaine 1967: 35-7.

O'Broin, Leon.   "An Dorchadas, An Original Play by Liam O'Flaherty." Fáinne an Lae 13 Márta 1926: 6.

Ó Buachalla, Breandán.   "Ó Cadhain, Ó Céileachair, Ó Flaithearta." Comhar Bealtaine 1967: 69-73.

Ó Ceallaigh, Caoimhin. "Cead Mile Failte Liam Ui Fhlaitheartaigh."
Feasta 38.7 (1985): 15.

---. "Liam O'Flaherty: Comharba Swift?" Feasta 38.10 (1985): 30.

Ó Cuagáin, Proinsias. "Dúil San Ainmhí Téama I Sgéalta Liam Ó
Flaithearta." Irisleabhar Mhá Nuad (1968): 49-59.

Ó hEithir, Breandán. "Liam Ó Flaithearta Agus a Dhúchas." Willie the
Plain Pint-Agus an Pápa. Baile Átha Cliath Agus Corcaigh: Cló
Mercier Teo., 1977. 65-76.

Sheeran, Pat. "Beastly Loot." Comhar 1984: 40-42.

Theo, "Dorchadas--Tuairim Eile." Fáinne an Lae 13 Márta 1926: 6.

(b) Books

Denvir, Gearóid. An Dúil is Dual. Indreabhán, Conamara: Cló Iar
Chonnachta Teo., 1991.

Ní Chéileachair, Síle. Dúil: Foclóir, Nótaí, Achoimre Agus Ceisteanna.
Baile Átha Cliath: Foilseacháin Náisiunta, 1981.

Ó Breatnach, Pádraig. Nótaí ar Dúil. Corcaigh: Cló Mercier Teo., 1971.

Ó Dúbhtaigh, Fiachra. Dúil Uí Fhlaithearta. Baile Átha Cliath:
Foilseacháin Náisiunta, 1981.

實踐大學數位出版合作系列
語言文學類　AG0113

Liam O'Flaherty: the Unromantic Seanchaí

作　　者	張婉麗
統籌策劃	葉立誠
文字編輯	王雯珊
視覺設計	賴怡勳
執行編輯	詹靚秋
圖文排版	陳湘陵
數位轉譯	徐真玉　沈裕閔
圖書銷售	林怡君
法律顧問	毛國樑　律師
發 行 人	宋政坤
出版印製	秀威資訊科技股份有限公司
	台北市內湖區瑞光路583巷25號1樓
	電話：(02) 2657-9211
	傳真：(02) 2657-9106
	E-mail：service@showwe.com.tw
經 銷 商	紅螞蟻圖書有限公司
	台北市內湖區舊宗路二段121巷28、32號4樓
	電話：(02) 2795-3656
	傳真：(02) 2795-4100
	http://www.e-redant.com

2009 年 7月
BOD 一版
定價：120元

讀　者　回　函　卡

感謝您購買本書,為提升服務品質,煩請填寫以下問卷,收到您的寶貴意見後,我們會仔細收藏記錄並回贈紀念品,謝謝!

1. 您購買的書名:_____

2. 您從何得知本書的消息?

　　□網路書店　□部落格　□資料庫搜尋　□書訊　□電子報　□書店

　　□平面媒體　□ 朋友推薦　□網站推薦　□其他_____

3. 您對本書的評價:(請填代號　1.非常滿意 2.滿意 3.尚可 4.再改進)

　　封面設計____　版面編排____　內容____　文/譯筆____　價格____

4. 讀完書後您覺得:

　　□很有收獲　□有收獲　□收獲不多　□沒收獲

5. 您會推薦本書給朋友嗎?

　　□會　□不會,為什麼?_____

6. 其他寶貴的意見:_____

_____

_____

_____

讀者基本資料

姓名:_____　年齡:_____　性別:□女 □男

聯絡電話:_____　E-mail:_____

地址:_____

學歷:□高中(含)以下　　□高中　　□專科學校　　□大學

　　　□研究所(含)以上 □其他_____

職業:□製造業 □金融業 □資訊業 □軍警 □傳播業 □自由業

　　　□服務業 □公務員 □教職　□學生 □其他_____

To：114

　　台北市內湖區瑞光路 583 巷 25 號 1 樓

　　秀威資訊科技股份有限公司　　　收

寄件人姓名：

寄件人地址：□□□

- -

(請沿線對摺寄回,謝謝!)

秀威與 BOD

BOD（Books On Demand）是數位出版的大趨勢，秀威資訊率先運用 POD 數位印刷設備來生產書籍，並提供作者全程數位出版服務，致使書籍產銷零庫存，知識傳承不絕版，目前已開闢以下書系：

一、BOD 學術著作—專業論述的閱讀延伸
二、BOD 個人著作—分享生命的心路歷程
三、BOD 旅遊著作—個人深度旅遊文學創作
四、BOD 大陸學者—大陸專業學者學術出版
五、POD 獨家經銷—數位產製的代發行書籍

BOD 秀威網路書店：www.showwe.com.tw
政府出版品網路書店：www.govbooks.com.tw

　　永不絕版的故事・自己寫・永不休止的音符・自己唱